The Cruz Chronicle

RUTGERS PRESS
fiction

The Cruz Chronicle

A Novel

Henry H. Roth

Rutgers University Press
New Brunswick and London

Portions of this novel, some in slightly different form, were previously published in *The Boston Review* (1972), *The Croton Review* (1978), *december* (1973), *Granite* (1977), *Latitudes Press* (1975), *Lillabulero Press* (1973), *The Little Magazine* (1973), *Ploughshares* (1974), *The Remington Review* (1976), *Seems* (1977), *A Shout in the Street* (1976), and *Works in Progress* (1973).

Library of Congress Cataloging-in-Publication Data

Roth, Henry H.
    The Cruz chronicle : a novel / by Henry H. Roth.
      p.   cm. — (Rutgers Press fiction)
    ISBN 0-8135-1404-5
    I. Title. II. Series.
    PS3568.O854C7   1989
    813'.54—dc19   88-28817
                                                                       CIP

British Cataloging-in-Publication information available

COPYRIGHT © 1989 BY RUTGERS, THE STATE UNIVERSITY
ALL RIGHTS RESERVED
MANUFACTURED IN THE UNITED STATES OF AMERICA

To, and for,

Sylvia

Contents

RAYMONDO CRUZ	*1*
JOSÉ	*13*
VICTOR	*29*
FELICIA	*41*
MOMMA	*51*
SWEET SATURDAY	*59*
THE WORD	*69*
THE BROTHERS AND MRS. MALLOY	*81*
FELIPE	*91*
MR. COLLISION	*97*
THE APARTMENT	*109*
THREE POINTS	*119*
CAPER	*133*
RAPPIN' WITH FELICIA	*147*
VICTOR'S DAMN LUCK	*155*
ASPECTS OF VICTOR CRUZ AT TWENTY-ONE	*165*
THE LONG WALK	*175*

The Cruz Chronicle

Raymondo Cruz

It's no understatement, only sad truth, that Raymondo Cruz's life did not begin until he died. Many years ago Raymondo, unable to provide even minimally for his family, tried to rob a bank with an empty water gun and was up-ended by a sharpshooting bank guard's stream of fat juicy bullets. Bleeding to death on a filthy West Side street, Raymondo heard a raucous hooting mob cheering his failure; the little man lay on his back mourning for his young sons—Victor, Felipe, and José—now alone and helpless with the evil and mad Maria Cruz. What a momma! The devil himself would have deserted such a woman, but Raymondo had stubbornly hung on trying to sustain his family. Now he thrashed grotesquely in a rich bloody stew, desperately sucking in air, choking on blood, trying to splatter the curious spectators. Then the crowd grew silent while the death rattle began.

Two days later, a brief funeral service was followed by an endlessly creaking drive to a desolate, weed-packed cemetery. The shabby coffin was yanked out of the battered Chevy station wagon and lugged up a hill overlooking a chemical waste landfill. However, Raymondo Cruz refused to greet death meekly like the usual bullet-riddled loser. In fact, he turned his back on the lousy fates and farted softly. Armed suddenly with tremendous willpower, the ghost of Raymondo Cruz would not simply rot in his pauper's grave. Instead, he exited long before the narrow hole had been fully topped by stony soil fill. And he vowed to watch over and tail his three sons forever.

Tranquil and very patient, the ghost of Raymondo Cruz sat on the busted curb across the street from his family. He scanned the filthy Bronx streets and gutted buildings he knew so well and waited for his role to begin.

It didn't take long for life with Maria Cruz to deteriorate even more. Early each morning, Victor fled to the streets and didn't return until bedtime. Maria rarely noticed his lengthy absences. The ghost of Raymondo Cruz was impressed by Victor's holding action. Only nine years old, the boy was wisest of his sons in addition to being the oldest. Victor's face had aged; he was learning that fate was not pleasant.

José, a sweet-faced five-year-old who still wet his pants, and Felipe, two years older and already sturdy as a body guard, stood on a rickety bridge chair, leaned out the windows waving at Victor, and eagerly followed their older brother's adventures during his long day. They too wished to escape. Tears circled Poppa's sad eyes. Victor entertained his captive audience by making funny faces and doing pratfalls. His brothers squealed with delight at such slapstick skills.

Soon, even sleeping in the apartment became an impossible task. The terrifying sounds of TV sets never turned off produced nights shaped by demons. Victor stole a pillow and a torn sheet, and luckily discovered an unbruised carton under a lamppost. The boy lugged his prize into a nearby alley, proceeded to swiftly gouge out windows and a small door, and using a fairly clean garbage-can cover, roofed his home. José and Felipe tossed down Magic Markers and crayons to brighten up the box. Victor graciously invited his brothers to a housewarming, but Momma had triple-locked all exit doors. Though pained by the events, Raymondo Cruz bided his time—really he had no other choice.

During a sudden rainstorm, the garbage-can cover loosened and, like a raft, swept down the avenue. A young cop found a soaked, feverish child amidst shredded cardboard and damp feathers. He carried Victor to a children's shelter. Once healthy again, the child was appointed a ward of the state.

When Victor, the eldest son, was dispatched by a wise children's court to Sacred Home for Fallen Angels, the father floated along and danced upon the roof of the bus hurtling upstate. Raymondo Cruz was overjoyed that Victor would grow up in the country prodded by nuns, amidst fresh air, with clean grass and pollen flying about like sweet litter. No city life for his son! Now if only José and Felipe could be so saved.

Patience, the ghost guided himself. Doing nothing is often better than doing something. I have learned that the very hard way.

Soon after Victor's arrival at Sacred Home for Fallen Angels, Poppa formally greeted his son. It was a windy cloudless day; the sky was a calm clear blue; and the crisp whispering grass seemed vacuumed and freshly dusted.

Victor immediately recognized his father's ghost and

was never frightened by the frail twisted body, riddled with bullet holes. Poppa's eyes and mouth were sculpted in amazement, for the ghost could never shake the trauma of death and still could not understand why the bank guard did not discover he bore only a water gun before the man permanently leveled him.

"This is our moment," Poppa said loudly.

Victor gulped and smiled dumbly. They shook hands and then embraced. Poppa felt cold and sweaty.

"You are the first of the Cruzes, and only you will ever be able to see and hear me."

"Thanks," Victor mumbled.

"I am only a maimed ghost. My powers are weak, Victor. Frankly it is a miracle that at least you can see me."

"It's ok, Poppa. It's fine," Victor soothed the ghost. He couldn't help staring at Poppa, who trembled with love and anxiety. Raymondo Cruz was shaking more than usual. Both he and Victor wished to cry, but they didn't.

Then Poppa suddenly talked firmly. "We must talk, Victor. You are still on probation here. You must learn to fit in."

Victor nodded. The ghost seemed exhausted.

"Are you ok, Poppa? Do you want to sit down?"

"I will never be ok, but today, with you, I am so much better."

Victor rubbed harshly at his eyes. His knees shook.

Poppa, clear-headed again, advised, "Do not fool or kid yourself, my son, there will be difficult times at this Sacred Home."

"Boy, I know it! I'm cutting classes now!"

The father, barely listening, continued, "Nuns are never armed with love and compassion. Victor, think of life here as a benign tumor, not a malignant one. You won't die of it and you won't be happy. You will be safe for a while. And you have never been safe before."

Victor was getting restless. It was great seeing Poppa again and knowing he would always be around. Still, he was getting restless.

"Write often to Felipe and José; inform them of your good news. Tell them how sad I am that my powers are limited, but I love them deeply. Explain there is hope for them, too."

Victor promised.

"I'm so proud you remembered me," Poppa confessed.

When the ghost of Raymondo Cruz vanished, Victor was truly impressed and began to feel a little more at ease at the sacred place he'd somehow lucked into.

Back in the Bronx, Maria Cruz neither clothed nor fed the two remaining brothers. Maria loved only TV. She bought set after set; all the welfare checks were used to purchase finer models. Maria had adamantly refused to send either Felipe or José to school.

"Never sleep, my children. You must guard, guard my new lovelies!" she warned. The brothers stayed slumped against the front door guarding the famed Maria Cruz TV collection from the countless Bronx thieves.

Oh, the ghost of Raymondo Cruz thought, how I wish I'd taken Maria along with me on the bank job. Then she'd be in some corner of hell, blind and deaf, surrounded by all the TVs in the world.

However, the ghost's continued patience was rewarded one very lucky day when Maria discovered watchdogs were even more efficient and economical than children. She purchased several ferocious beasts, and there in her apartment, surrounded by mounds of dog shit and the clamor of countless TVs, she watched, listened, and calmly spent her life. Maria Cruz surrendered Felipe and José to the court and then to Sacred Home. The ghost of Raymondo Cruz now had his family under one Christian roof. He often tiptoed into some drafty church to give thanks.

Even after Felipe and José arrived at the institution, only Victor was blessed with the gift of being with Poppa. The other brothers never doubted their older brother's vision. Happily they always passed along their love to Poppa and were truly proud that someone still cared for them—even though it was a ghost. And the old man's advice was sound, practical, often curt. The ghost never raised his voice in admonishment, so for a long time Victor listened and didn't mind the old man repeating himself.

"Never carry a gun, allow no bulges in your pockets, and try not to look forbidding. Break as few rules as possible, and if caught, confess and suck ass unashamedly. Warn and inform your brothers. Sacred Home is like a hotel with bad service. Bad, maybe even lousy cruel service; but it's not the Bronx, and a hotel is a hotel. Read the *Daily News!*" All the brothers liked that gossip and agreed with such deep truths.

Victor was a primitive child, and not given to slyness in his outrages against society. He was guilty as hell each time, and usually got caught red-handed. Before he was twelve Victor had stolen and crashed two cars, threatened an assistant principal at Sacred Home, and set fire to a lumberyard. His father's teaching saved him: Victor always confessed and happily admitted full guilt. He would beg the head of the Home, Sister Noreen, to forgive him. Victor would roll on the floor epileptically with an erection, added proof of the intensity of his feelings. The old, cruel nun, withered and fierce, melted like a wax candle before the humble Puerto Rican groveling at her high-buttoned shoes. Victor was promptly forgiven, chastised, almost kissed, and sent back to prey on society.

In adolescence, Victor calmed down, became more solid and straight with each passing year. It was as if the ghost's presence, words, and advice wore Victor down and muffled the young man. Victor had a poor memory and was not glib or eager to talk too long, so many of Raymondo's best bits were shortened or lost in translation. Therefore, Poppa only wished for more direct contact with Felipe and José who now wildly roamed the grounds of Sacred Home for Fallen Angels.

The old man was pleased by the differences in his three sons. Similarities and love bound them, yet it was the differences that made the Cruzes; they had faults to be sure, but only the blind and the jealous would dare deny that Victor, José, and Felipe possessed singular talents.

José Cruz was the youngest, the smartest, the most mischievous, and a truly fabulous organizer: a pusher by the time he was twelve and at fourteen prince pimp for the Home girls who gave themselves (no longer freely) to high school boys from a neighboring state.

If Victor was becoming boring and plodding, and José evolving into a wise and oily rapper, then Felipe was the Cruz bodyguard. Very powerful and tall, Felipe protected his brothers from physical attacks and verbal sniping. Once a cottage-mate innocently gossiped about seeing the Cruz brothers waving and talking into the thin air and shouting praise to someone named Poppa. That boy sucked his food through a straw for more than six months and remained forever toothless.

While Felipe and José were hanging on at the Sacred

Home by the skin of their elbows, Victor had graduated, nailed a construction job and secured his first junky apartment not far from the shopping mall that he was helping to build. The ghost of Raymondo Cruz could hardly complain, for he was very fortunate to have survived an abrupt end of life and still be around. Yet he bitched plenty and experienced moments of depression. Even a ghost grows old and more sad and lonely. In truth, the old man's existence wasn't much. He wore the same suit every day: a cheap black suit with a stained burgundy vest and pointed tap shoes. The old man was getting bald and his hands shook.

"I have been a failure, I know," the old man wailed, after he had drunk out of too many paper bags. "If the bank job had been ok, we would be living in a fine house in Queens. Now all my sons may soon be out on the streets, even though this is the suburbs. You, Victor, should be in a fine house, not an apartment." The ghost of Raymondo Cruz openly wept. Proud and a little amazed by his good luck in finding any apartment, Victor dutifully tried to flash a big grin and calm down the anguished ghost, who was swiftly ruining his good mood.

Victor said softly, "I speak for all of us, Poppa. Nah, nah, Pop, you did good. You always tried. We appreciate it. Soon we'll show you how much we appreciate it. Look, don't cry. We're still a family."

Victor worked on a construction gang assembling new stores in an area where parking had replaced all trees and flowers. When he discovered they were building a bank, Victor dedicated a special nook of the brick facade, whispering, "For my father, Raymondo Cruz, I consecrate this shitty corner."

Victor had learned that, unbelievably, there was no night watchman at the site. He had overheard an electrician complaining that the burglar system was not yet installed, though the bank was fat with money and would open in three days with a fancy premiere. Then Victor told his brothers how their father's untimely death would be avenged; the ghost of Raymondo Cruz would weep no more. Soon the Cruz family could have the fine mansion with big juicy cars spread out under fresh air and clean stars.

Raymondo Cruz did not accompany his family to the bank robbery that night. He longed to go, but could not. Even now, Raymondo's body trembled when he recalled the fiery pellets entering and vacating his guts.

"Don't worry, Pop. It's in the bag," Victor bragged.

But it wasn't in the bag though mighty Felipe Cruz tore out the loose bricks from Victor's special corner and they were inside. So quickly were the Cruz bunch viciously assaulted by seven savage attack dogs, there was no time to shout a single cry of pain. The dogs were the first pure litter from Maria Cruz, who had taken to breeding superb killer dogs to finance her TV habit.

Raymondo Cruz, who had been drawn to the bank by a sudden foreboding, saw the blood draining off the newly tarred bank driveway. He slipped through the walls and came upon his battered sons. The dogs slunk to the basement, where safe-deposit boxes were neatly stacked. In the eerie silence Poppa heard the animals cleaning themselves. Like a master craftsman, he gently repaired and attended to his sons' wounds. The dogs began howling softly while the ghost of Raymondo Cruz made three trips carrying his wounded home.

They recuperated slowly at Victor's pad and Raymondo Cruz did not orate any "I-told-you-so's." He graciously thanked Victor for his valiant vindication attempt. He let matters rest until his sons' wounds were almost healed, and then Poppa whispered softly to Victor, "Pain and pleasure are very close sins. Better to lose those senses." Victor sighed and groaned in his tormented sleep. Poppa was sure the boy had heard and only hoped he would understand and not forget the meaning.

To himself Raymondo muttered, Love and meddling can truly save one's ass. What brutal fate might have overtaken the Cruzes if Raymondo had not tailed his three brave sons! Sleep, he blessed the crowded room of Cruz wounded, and then he, too, tried to nap.

Humming continuously, the ghost of Raymondo Cruz poured chunky herbs and grainy spices into pots of cloudy boiling water. To Victor his eldest son he promised, "Drink this potion hourly and your wounds will be shut tight, like the doors of the rich."

Groggy with pain, Victor asked, "Are you a witch doctor, too?"

Poppa looked forlorn. "Your mother's friend, Estrella, is the witch and false prophet. Trust my cooking. Never before was I able to care for my sons."

"Sure, sure." Victor began dozing off.

Poppa walked about the quiet apartment mumbling, "In an illness at the right moment all barriers vanish."

Two massive pots trembled on the shaky gas stove. The flames were never shut off. After a while Poppa even stopped adding ingredients; still the brew never dwindled. José, Felipe, and Victor not only healed quickly, but any blemishes were erased and their skins became dewy like babies'. The steam from the pots completely warmed the usually chilly apartment. Never had the apartment seemed more like a home. All the brothers were impressed.

José said happily, "Boy, Poppa really saved our asses. I feel like a new man."

Victor grumbled, "And he's never going to let us forget it."

José

Once they were healed, Victor and Felipe found crap work. José never even considered searching for employment. The youngest Cruz only dreamed of Momma. Every few days he snuck away and ended up in the Bronx with Maria Cruz for a couple of hours.

One evening a few weeks later, over a dinner of pork fried rice, egg rolls, and orange soda, Felipe stared angrily at José's dreamy look.

"Now what you mooning about, José."

"I miss Poppa's soup. We shoulda bottled some of that soup."

Victor, ignoring them both, was hunched over the table writing a note to Poppa.

Felipe asked, "Why? We don't need it now."

José sneered, "Victor, you hear Felipe? He doesn't understand the meaning of planning. What if we got banged up again?"

Felipe butted in. "Then stay home more, wise guy, and cook it up."

JOSÉ

Victor wrote to Poppa, "I know you saved us good, Poppa, but I got to see you and soon. You must be tired of playing nursemaid, but come. It's real important."

A few days later, Poppa floated above Victor. Victor impatiently motioned him to sit down. Poppa remained floating. Victor sighed.

Poppa saw the boy had a perplexed look and the ghost asked "Is there bad news?"

"It's about Momma."

The ghost said formally, "I'd rather never speak about her."

"Me either, but José don't feel that way. That's the problem. What can we do?"

"Nothing."

"Huh?"

"Some are lucky with their mommas and wives. Not the Cruzes."

"We got to make some plan, Poppa. Hey, don't drift off. You grew up with her, right? You were childhood pals, right?"

"Yes," Raymondo Cruz sighed.

When Maria was a teenager, she began tattooing her lovely body with religious slogans. Raymondo Cruz was no seminary student, but young, romantic, and stupid. He took her good-looking face and wily shape and thought fine, fine stuff. But he was wrong, wrong. In the beginning, at noisy parties and in the crowded lobby of the local movie palace, they often eyed each other like horny prizefighters. Then, while sauntering down the street together one cool, breezy, smelly, moon-soaked evening, Maria stopped and leaned against a parked car. It was unlocked, and she demurely went inside. Of course, Raymondo followed. It was their finest moment, and despite his lousy memory, Raymondo recalled every fabulous initial love stroke and thrust. The ghost of Raymondo Cruz sympathized with José's fascination and crazy optimism, but there was only madness in that Bronx apartment. Maria was still shapely, but she gave off a burnt-out odor, and the place smelled like a filthy prehistoric marsh.

"Poppa, are you listening?"

"Yes, yes."

"How do we keep José away from the Bronx and her? That punk gets into more than enough messes in the country. In the Bronx, he's dead."

"José lost something he never had. He knows that, but checks it out anyway," Raymondo explained.

"But that's crazy, huh. C'mon, are you drunk?"

"A family conference is a special occasion. It is never meant for anger or quick decisions. Be patient and try to meet all the sides."

"What fucking sides? José should stay away from her!"

Poppa said softly, "For José it's impossible to truly give her up. I can understand, Victor."

"You too, Poppa, you too go back?"

"No, my son," the ghost sighed.

"Sometimes I think José might stay there with her. Then what?"

"We would go into the Bronx and save him. But have no fear. José is our youngest. He longs for happy endings."

Victor roared, "No fucking way!"

Once Mamma invited them to the Bronx for Thanksgiving dinner. Victor had just graduated from Sacred Home and was looking for a decent place in the country. Felipe and José hadn't flunked out yet.

The dog shit had been cleared from the dining room. José and Victor and Felipe were the only guests. Also present were Momma, a sensational turkey with side

JOSÉ

dishes of tasty beans, rice, crisp fried bananas, plus fresh fruit soaked in sangria, lots of walnuts, and plenty of beer, soda, tea, and coffee. All the brothers were quiet, like it was the last supper, and José was asked a couple of times in mumbling whispers to please pass the salt. Victor had cried openly twice during the fucking meal. Later, when the brothers were taking off, Momma told them now that they were growing up, she expected half their weekly salaries.

"I never went back. And even Felipe knows enough to stay away," Victor said proudly.

"But you can't order José to keep away."

"Hey, I know that. Then the kid would go back every day and twice on Sunday. Still, I'm plenty worried!"

"Be of good cheer. José is safe."

"Jeez, you can't be that sure! She's a witch. José says there's a new baby and a new lousy boyfriend. Poppa, the baby cries all the time like we did."

The ghost of Raymondo Cruz trembled and wished to flee, but bravely stayed put and pointed out, "José finds nothing at the lost and found, so quickly returns to the country. He always leaves her, Victor."

"So far, Poppa."

"Always," the ghost assured Victor, who seemed exhausted by the discussion. And the family conference was over.

The bank where Poppa was shot was in the basement of the fattest and most impressive building José Cruz had ever seen. The lowest floor contained a bakery, a dry cleaner, a stationery store, and a supermarket. It was like a built-in shopping mall. Since the building was old and grimy, the guy who had planned the operation was smart as a prophet. Everything was in easy reach, no tenant need ever leave the apartment house. And across the street was a damn funeral parlor.

In his dreams, José had often circled the block and bank, but he had never showed up before. Today he went right into the Chemical Bank like anybody else, nudging the revolving door only a little bit in order to delay his entrance an extra second.

"Was there ever a robbery here?" he asked a dozing guard.

"Uh, yeah."

"When?"

"Once, kid. A real long time ago. They never tried again."

"Were you here then?"

He leaned against the desk with all the paper and pens, his beefy shadow elbowing the faggy desk.

"Did you stop the robbery? How many were there?"

"There was only one."

"Did . . . ?"

"Yeah, I shot the guy, kid."

"Was it exciting? Do you still think about it?"

"Hell, nobody asked me. You're a funny kid, what do you care?"

"Do you still dream about it?"

"What the hell do you care?"

"I fucking care, man!"

"Look, I'm still on duty. I'm supposed to move around, help people."

"You're supposed to answer questions."

"About the bank, sonny."

"I'm asking about the bank, man! Did you kill the guy?"

"Well, here it is, Mr. Curious. He was a small guy,

not old, but tough and mean and he came in swearing and smoking a thin cigar and he had a tommy-gun barking. Lucky no one else was killed. I told everyone to hit the floor and I shot him six times in the gut. Now beat it."

"You fuck. You fucking liar, he only had a water gun, just a bean shooter, you prick!"

"Hey!"

"*Hey* is for horses, you fat pig! Look out, cop. I'm going to get you one day. I'm Raymondo Cruz's son!"

"C'mere, c'mere!"

Momma was so proud, hugging José, telling him he did the right thing by only threatening the guy.

"Now he'll be nervous every time somebody taps him on the shoulder for a bank question."

Momma and her gypsy cohort Estrella promised to put a strong hex on the bastard.

A month later, Momma caught the flu and couldn't pick up her welfare check. When José visited her, she sent him to social services. It seemed like an easy mission as he rode a beat-up bike into the dingy lobby. But a goddamn young cop told him to get his bike the hell back on the street.

José politely ignored the advice and sped down the dimly lit halls. Hand on holster, the cop darted in pursuit. José only thought, Wow, me and Poppa—the real desperadoes. Caught near a malfunctioning water fountain, José played dumb, telling the racist cop he couldn't speak English. But the cop was furious and didn't care how dumb his captive was. He kicked the frail bike, forcing José to defend himself. The cop fell and José rode the bruised bike back and forth on the bully's knuckles until more cops arrived. They found a knife on José and the young cop, sucking his knuckles like he was sucking pussy, was very happy.

"A knife is a felony, kid. Also resisting arrest and harassing a policeman are felonies, kid."

"I'm a whittler."

Furious that José could speak English and knew a big word, the cop really leveled him, then his knights joined in and worked the boy over. José kept yelling he was a whittler and they should call his gallery.

José once told the chief psychiatrist at the Sacred Home for Fallen Angels about dreaming. The doc had almost called for the butterfly net.

"See, I dream all right, but I'm never in the dreams. In real life I can look into a mirror and never see me."

Linda Cohen, the art therapist, noted José's poor self-image, and encouraged him to paint portraits, but none of the faces were his and she'd tease, "Where are you, José Cruz?"

"I'm here, art lady, *here.*"

So when the nosy cop found the knife, José flashed back to the art room and pictured Linda all right, and shouted a word he never knew, "Whittler! I'm a damn whittler, you dumb pig."

A confident civil liberties attorney named Marty Halloran promised José he could beat the rap "if we can find a gallery to agree you're a whittler." José smiled a lot and left it all up to Halloran, "my attorney."

Halloran ordered him to paint and draw like hell and got José's finished work accepted into a community-sponsored art show. In court, Halloran presented a local newspaper ad to the judge with José Cruz's name, and a hundred others, mostly bored housewives, whose works had appeared in the crummy show.

JOSÉ

The county attorney for the cops said, "So what, it's not whittling."

But Halloran had his opponent by the nuts. "His knife was taken, your honor, and he naturally turned to another art form."

Even the red-faced judged smiled, suddenly on the side of creativity, though he never looked at the artist, only at Halloran.

That was ok, because he said real loud, "Counselor, see to it that your client does not turn back to whittling." And the case was dismissed for lack of evidence.

Of course Victor and Felipe were happy to see José beat the rap, but these days Victor was always straight and serious.

"OK, little brother, you got lucky, now stick to a job. We need money every day, José."

"Look, Victor, I do my thing, you do yours."

"You start looking for work tomorrow."

Felipe said, "Women are crazy about you, lover. You ought to have them hustle for you."

"Jerk, I ain't exploiting anybody anymore, and nobody exploits me either."

Victor shouted, "All you do is make speeches! Shut up!"

As soon as his brothers left for the day, José stole a couple of bucks from Victor's drawer and bussed back into the city. Every time he left the country, there was this creepy feeling when the bus made the wide turn and headed for the Bronx and Momma.

Momma never mourned Raymondo's death one goddamned second. She buried him all right, but she never paid the oily undertaker, Julio. To this day Julio gossiped about and cursed her family, and swore openly that he would never bury any new Cruzes until the old bill was paid.

Here was a momma who spoke Latin, Greek, and French when she was obsessed and the devil lurked in her guts—like some educated weirdo had massaged her brain—and she blurted out nutty words only a professor could understand and marvel at. Once the fit was over, Momma couldn't remember anything. For a long time, José was scared shitless, but once he got used to her ravings it was like seeing a miracle. All the other times Momma was just a lousy mother battering her kids, never feeding them or buying clothes, only adding more TVs to her collection. Her garbage was continually cluttered with discarded sets and tubes.

José opened Momma's bathroom and released a mob of roaches. Some fat daddies lagged behind, daring any human to be quick and strong enough to smash them. José never backed off a challenge and got a few juicy kills. Momma slapped him, but not too hard, because he was definitely her favorite.

"José," she warned, "roaches are not to be killed."

He stared hard at Momma—the lady who years ago booted the brothers out of the South Bronx, over the Hudson River, and into the Sacred Home of Fallen Angels. She never once visited in all the years they rotted there. Still, every time José looked at her he could bawl. Once or twice he did, for you only get one momma, no matter how lousy she may be. Why expect compassion from a momma who packed them all away without a mothball; who lay down for anyone with half a cock; and who helped kill Poppa, driving him so wild the poor guy tried to rob a bank with a water gun.

He tried to be the good son. "How about if I spray poison in the cabinet and rub 'em out?"

JOSÉ

She slammed him harder this time. This one José felt to the soles of his Adidases.

Maria chanted fiercely in a sing-song voice, "You can hear them talk. Listen, roaches are all one family. All are friends and very happy. They ain't just dumb bugs. They're smarter than my watch dogs."

"Momma, Momma, your dogs are trained to watch color TVs. Even a social worker could understand protecting private property. It's in the Constitution. But what good is a roach?"

Momma shouted, "Don't mock me, I don't speak good English. Estrella says it better—roaches have places in the universe. When one is murdered like you just done, it's reborn into a dozen other roaches bigger and stronger and nastier. You keep killing them and they'll take over. You best let them die natural. Estrella is a wise gypsy lady. She knows the future, José!"

Estrella, the retarded gypsy, would lay a roach if it got a welfare check, José thought unkindly.

"You love roaches better than me!"

She warned, "Don't kill 'em here or in your own house."

Momma was getting that far-away look.

José asked softly, "How do they talk, Momma?"

He was ready to duck because she was holding a frying pan and was inches away from a big kitchen knife, but she smiled like some sweet old saint and answered sweetly, very sweetly, "They got deep voices like the colored and they mumble a lot."

Lovingly, Momma patted her newest set, a nineteen-inch Sony.

Then she said, "I'm only buying color now. Nobody buys black and white, José." She was even smaller than

José. She looked like a pretty jockey. Though she was getting really old, her eyes were still wild like a girl's, but there were deep lines down from her nice eyes and into her thin lips. Today she wore rags, looked like a damn beggar, and was carrying a wailing baby. Her latest boyfriend slept loudly on the couch.

Maria pointed to the man and whispered, "Make no noise. He needs his sleep. He is a master TV repair craftsman."

José's new step-brother looked worse than all her brood put together. Puerto Rican all right, but his skin was bruised blue. Momma guessed what he was thinking.

"I never hit this one. I tell you it's my favorite. But he's been sick. Been sick for weeks."

"Take him to the fucking doctor."

"I'll cure him, but I been busy."

So he got out fast and headed for the Bronx Zoo where it smelled better and animals were in cages and fed. That baby will die before I make it home again, José thought helplessly. It's like my life, a very small busted bridge going nowhere. I take one tiny step and that's it, it's over. No wonder I don't want to see who I am or what I'm wrestling, and how do I know if I'm winning, even a little bit? Frightened, José ran out of the zoo toward a subway station. He popped in his token, boarded a filthy train, and headed for the bus terminal.

Country buses were fast. Even rich white men used them to get back and forth from the cushy city jobs. Patches of sunlight grazed his window. Whenever José was this gloomy, he couldn't even see the guy sitting next to him. Feeling lodged in a deep dark box, José knew a man was there but couldn't tell the color of the sap's overcoat. Forlorn, José envied these confident passengers heading to cozy nests, for he'd never had a sure way home, ever. Whenever he was this bad he thought of that terrific Linda Cohen, the only Jew who ever worked at the Sacred Home and was always a friend. He remembered her inviting them over for supper, and how she fought to keep all the Cruzes in school. She won only with dumb Victor. And then her husband had to relocate to California and she had to go and take care of her own kids. Linda still wrote. Twice the brothers had called collect, and she was really happy to hear from them.

Felipe and Victor were already eating.

"Why are you late, José?"

"School out late?" Felipe teased.

"Fuck you," José snapped.

Only tuna fish on the table. The older brothers were mad as hell because he hadn't stayed home to cook something hot. José had just sat down when the doorbell rang. Shit!

Smiling, Mr. Halloran followed by two fat old clowns in matching trenchcoats walked into the apartment. It couldn't be the damn judge had changed his mind since Halloran was smiling.

"José Cruz, this is Mr. and Mrs. Golden." Halloran was the first decent Irish guy José ever met, and now here were two Jews who must be his friends.

Victor waved and raced into the kitchen to boil hot water. Felipe just nodded and grabbed José's lousy supper portion.

"Well," Halloran said, "I just wanted you to know immediately what's happened. I'm so happy and proud, José."

"So are we, Mr. Halloran and Mr. Cruz," the couple chimed in.

"Huh?"

"José, they've seen your paintings at the County Art Show and bought one, and the art center won't take a fee, so the money is all yours."

Mr. Golden looked like he wanted to make a speech, but José flashed him a mugging scowl and his patron just handed over a check for two hundred dollars for doing nothing. Victor lugged in a huge kettle of boiling water and asked who wanted coffee or tea. The Goldens didn't want a beverage. In fact, they looked a little scared. Mr. Halloran still smiled, though.

"Isn't that terrific, José?"

"Great, great, thanks."

"Thank *you*, young man," the old lady spoke for the first time, and then the Goldens got the hell out, brushing off their trenchcoats all the way.

Victor asked, "How much?"

José remembered the art lady explaining how the artist is exploited because he's usually trusting.

José thought, Exploit me, who gives a fuck, but let me sleep tomorrow.

"Two hundred dollars. Now lay off me for a few days. Here, take it for the rent, Victor."

The next morning Victor pocketed the check and ordered, "You've got to work, c'mon." They had their coats on and were waiting. José reached for his windbreaker.

"Hey, where you going? You're not going anywhere."

"Then why'd you wake me?"

Felipe warned, "You start painting now, we got you another piece of paper."

"Canvas, you moose," Victor corrected.

And Victor soothed, "You work hard and stop about four and cook the chicken. Ok, little brother?"

"Yeah, sure."

In this great dream I'm walking on a canvas road that stretches forever. It's really comfortable and spongy. There's some shape I can see walking on the canvas. I may be able to see myself for the very first time. Just then, I'm dumped off the couch and that's good-bye dream. Felipe is grinning like the dumb fuck he is. I try to kick him but, as usual, Felipe dodges.

I go right back to sleep and see the figure again walking, it's the same damn dream. The guy has a giant Magic Marker, and he writes his name on the road like a big shot. Beautiful handwriting and it's me, all right. My ass is in my face, but I can see the signature—JOSÉ CRUZ. I wait and wait and then I write under the name "artist proof."

But I have no damn skills, can't rumble with Felipe's punch, and don't have the luck of Victor, who can rap with the dead past and be pals with Poppa. Long, long ago I asked Victor, "Does Poppa look all right?" but he thought I was teasing and ordered Felipe to kick the shit out of me. And once I asked Momma, "Did Poppa ever go on a vacation?" She laughed like a hyena and told me how he'd been to the Bronx Zoo and bought a hot dog and peanuts, and once he went to Yankee Stadium to see baseball. That was his vacation, taking off his shirt on a cloudy day to see some dummies play a game.

I miss him still and would like to know more about his life or just plain see Raymondo Cruz. I wish I could remember anything about him. I'm going to speak to

Victor again about Poppa. I want to know how wonderful it was when the first bullet hit and he knew it was all over. Is the pain sweet pleasure? And when the sixth bullet cuddles inside do you discover, even for a second, paradise? Wasn't it great, Poppa, to know you'd never really have to see us or her again? And do you realize what a hero you are to still follow us?

I'm going to write down lots more questions for Victor to ask.

Victor

Early one morning before Victor left for work, Poppa joined him at the breakfast table.

"Don't let money swim to your head and heart," advised the ghost of Raymondo Cruz.

"I don't make that kind of money, Poppa, c'mon."

"A man is never judged by money alone, especially by his loved ones."

"Sit down, Poppa. You make me nervous bouncing off the walls like that."

"*I* am the nervous one."

How could any father not be proud of his sons' stumbling foray into the world? Yet, the ghost of Raymondo Cruz was ambivalent in his happiness. As he had warned, pleasure was to be avoided at all costs. Don't get him wrong; he was *pleased.* No son was in prison yet, and they had definitely banded together in a prime assault on survival. However, Victor's construction job—true, he was only a laborer—netted the boy twice what Raymondo had ever earned weekly as a janitor for the tenement they once inhabited. Despite himself, despite all the new wisdom he had picked up, there was painful jealousy budding in Raymondo's broken body now that Victor had so easily assumed the role of the head man and sole provider.

The father erotically mused: it is much like if Victor were to make love to a big star like Cher. Then I the poppa would be proud and boastful, but also long to replace my son and be locked in this woman's embrace. The past seemed very immediate and paraded by in monstrous shapes. So Raymondo Cruz dropped out of sight and drifted upstate for a while.

Victor was not surprised that the old man disappeared for weeks. When his brothers kept asking about Poppa, Victor softly replied, "Maybe he met himself a fine-looking lady ghost, huh?"

Victor loved construction work. He took enormous pleasure and pride in being sweaty, tired, and dirty. Once home he'd take a couple of hot showers, then strut around the living room in clean t-shirt and briefs, sipping wine, smoking grass, and eating what José prepared. Since being drop-kicked out of the Home, José half-heartedly cooked and tidied the apartment. And Felipe did the dishes and took out the garbage.

Too quickly summer and fall were over and the sky turned black and rotten. It was cold as hell. There were layoffs and men without seniority were released after a second consecutive subfreezing day. It broke Victor's heart when he was dropped.

José, whose only goal was to be a troublemaker, giggled, "I told you, Victor, you and the spades are the last to be hired and the first to be fired!" Victor slammed the boy in the gut.

"I wasn't *fired*, fag, I was laid off."

Victor had saved enough money to pay another two months' rent, but there was to be no more straight grocery shopping, only rip-offs.

"You got to steal more, José."

José giggled, "Ok, ok, don't get mad, Victor. Just don't let dummy Felipe come along with me. Once he walks into a supermarket they close it up."

None of the boys looked for work. Gloomily, Victor watched TV all day, but still he didn't understand how his mother could do this twenty years in a row and why she required a dozen working sets. The apartment became cluttered. Victor had never realized how inadequate the damn place was—like a fucking submarine out of old war movies where everyone starts to get on everyone else's nerves and then suddenly they sink a Jap battleship and the crew is happy and content.

Victor intentionally picked fights with Felipe and José, who joined sides to beat him down. Twice the Russian landlord, Kousitsky, warned them to cut the racket. Victor knew it was mostly his fault, but he couldn't stop himself. He was on a long, elaborate slide into failure and right on target until he awoke to discover on the edge of the bed, patiently waiting for him to awake, a beaming Raymondo Cruz.

Poppa was very happy. The room had the familiar stink of poverty, and the damn reeky sweat of frustration.

The ghost of Raymondo Cruz bathed luxuriously for a moment in such pathos and then advised, "Look, it's icy as hell. Outside, accidents are a dime a dozen. Think of all the lousy drivers out here in the country!"

Victor was edgy. Felipe and José were demanding to sleep in the good bed now that Victor was just another loafer.

"So, my son," Raymondo continued, "head for a wreckage shop. You will easily find work. All my boys are gifted with their hands."

And it was true. José could strip the well-dressed of their personal belongings in seconds, and Felipe was

VICTOR

often sought as a bouncer at the livelier discos on Saturday nights and holidays. The old man smiled, embraced Victor, and disappeared. Victor roughly awoke José and ordered him to make breakfast. José leaped to the task when he heard the old Victor Cruz voice, loud and mean with nasty power and drive.

"José, where's Felipe?"

"I dunno. He didn't come home last night."

"Hell, where'd he go? He's been disappearing all week."

"Last night, late, someone visited, then Felipe said good night. I think he took your coat. But he left cash for the rent! How about that?"

"Not great," Victor scowled.

"Hey, c'mon, the big turkey saved the day. Why aren't you happy? You jealous?"

Victor shook his head. "I'm getting nervous and scared. How can that chump have a fat wallet? Who'd he go off with?"

José said, "I don't know."

"Who do you think it was?"

"Probably Lopez."

Victor snapped his fingers and clenched and unclenched his fists.

"Sure! That bum deals hard stuff and he's fucking stupid; done time already."

"Lopez is not that dumb. You see his shoes and car? Felipe and him are close now. Relax, big brother."

"I'm dealing with Felipe, now," Victor promised.

José asked, "How many eggs you want scrambled?"

"As many as are in the fridge, little brother."

Brio Auto Body Works welcomed Victor with open, wily arms. Augie Brio hired only those clearly in dire straits, so twenty down-and-outers were paid less in wages than seven skilled collision experts commanded.

Augie asked Victor, "You come from that Sacred Home?"

"I got out couple of years ago."

"Thrown out, huh?" Augie had asked good-naturedly.

"No man, I graduated high school. I don't have no high school equivalency thing. I got a diploma." Victor snapped.

"Oh, great, kid. You'll work six days a week and help fix my house every other Sunday and you'll get $150 a week."

Victor looked for his father, but like all poor advisers and incorrect prophets, the ghost had vanished.

"Sure, Mr. Brio," Victor said softly, "Thanks a lot, Mr. Brio." Thanks for screwing me.

Here was a new, terrible kind of exploited weariness. Sometimes Victor was so exhausted, he fell asleep in his clothes the moment he was back inside the apartment. Once he napped beside some wheels he was realigning. Augie booted him into alertness and cautioned that the next time he'd dock his pay. Back in the apartment, Victor wearily recounted his long day.

"He's a fascist, racist pig," José announced. "Felipe ought to wreck Brio's whole body."

Felipe leaned against the living room wall as if he were Eddie Murphy. He'd suddenly become smug, arrogant, and rich, but no smarter. Now Felipe was always dressed in sporty new clothes, and he'd bought several fancy pairs of shoes. Since he'd paid last month's rent, Felipe now slept in the former bed of Victor Cruz.

"Where you collect all that green, Felipe?" José asked.

Felipe pulled out a cigar and waved it around like a baton.

"None of your business, retard."

José said weakly, "I gotta paint some more and win some prizes."

"Take you a hundred years to make money like I do," Felipe sneered.

"Just what do you do?" Victor inquired softly.

"Easy, easy stuff. Who needs to sweat like you in construction or auto body. Shit, that's for peasants!"

José grinned, "Felipe, you ain't smart enough to even be a peasant."

Felipe lumbered toward him. "Who says so?"

José was ready to duck, but Felipe dismissed him with a limp wave and began to lovingly pat his checkered sports jacket. Finally Felipe spat out, "And whoever's ripping off my after-shave cologne, better fucking cut it out."

Victor knew it was useless, but warned Felipe anyway, "If you only work a few hours a week, it can't be *legal*."

But Felipe knew it all, ignored Victor, and resumed leaning against the wall.

Now Poppa was showing up all the damn time.

The ghost of Raymondo Cruz cautioned Victor, "No, my son, don't worry if the dirt is embedded in your fingernails. You are not a dandy, but a collision repairman. Wear your bruises and dirt proudly as a badge."

"That fucking Brio cheats me. I am worth three times what he pays."

"It's true of many who work."

"Brio collects losers and dumps on them."

"You have no choice. Even if it's shoveling shit, a man must work."

"I am not ashamed of being Puerto Rican. I am not even ashamed of you," Victor blurted out.

"Patience, patience. Two bad seasons will be followed by five good ones."

"And Felipe may be in jail by the end of the month. Money has swollen his head, Poppa."

VICTOR

"You've warned Felipe not to carry a gun or anything that resembles a gun?"

"Of course."

"It bears repeating. He is a Cruz. He knows our family tragedy; he must not carry a gun. How I wish the other boys too could see me! But you are the eldest, Victor; you must do what you can."

Victor had really begun to understand that being a ghost had not changed poor Poppa at all. He was like any other weak father.

On Friday, only Victor was not paid. He waited impatiently as other meek mechanics trooped home. He and Brio were alone in the smoky shop.

"I'll pay you Sunday, baby. I want us to have a long talk."

"You getting ready to fire me?"

"Hey, you're the best of the twenty I got. Smile, kiddo. I'm going to make you an offer. You tell your landlord you'll pay him Sunday night."

Augie shot off the master lightswitch and shoved Victor outside. For a crazy blinding instant Victor was going to hurl himself at the man, take the one hundred-fifty bucks and a couple of hundred more for the weeks he'd been cheated. He'd already decided it would be a stupid move when Poppa's bad breath enveloped him.

"Easy, my son, easy. Two bad seasons will be followed by five good ones."

Augie Brio was safely in his Caddy, swerving away. Victor walked the damn two miles in the freezing cold to the apartment.

On Sunday he painted the bathroom. Mrs. Brio loved the color and then Augie threw his dumpy wife and three dumpy kids out of the house, ordering them to go find a hamburger place or have a pizza.

VICTOR

He said to Victor, "Hey, c'mon in the living room."

Nothing in the freaking living room but a shellacked floor, a skinny flowered couch, and a glass coffee table with nothing on it. There were plenty of other rooms, but less furniture than the Cruz boys had fitted into their dump. Maybe Augie wasn't making a bundle. Still, the Italian looked and smelled rich.

"How many jobs you had?"

"I was never fired."

"Don't be nervous, just tell me how many."

"I worked in a laundry at the Home, then I was a dishwasher, a short-order cook, and I helped build the Mall. Now I'm in auto body."

"All are hard jobs. Some day soon, Victor, you're going to have it soft."

Victor only belched, sighed, and waited. The ghost of Raymondo Cruz sat in a corner of the room also waiting.

"Somebody's fucking me up in the shop. Parts of good cars break down. Ten times is no accident."

"Maybe you got enemies."

"Oh, I got *them*, all right. And *one extra* in my body shop I didn't know about. I trust you, kid. You'll make a good foreman some day. You check it out for me."

"Hey, I . . ."

"It'll mean a raise of ten bucks a week, and an extra fifty when you nail the wise guy. I could catch the prick eventually, but it'd take me more time. You should handle it by the end of next week."

"I'll try."

"Awright!"

During the long walk back home, the ghost of Raymondo Cruz matched his son stride for stride.

"Are you going to give yourself up?" he inquired. "I like to see men work and sweat. You do sensational work, but you also sabotage cars."

36

Victor nodded, "Nah, I won't give myself up. There's one special white pig José would order Felipe to stomp. I think I'll say it's him."

"I have failed as a father," the ghost wailed.

"Wrong. You taught how important it is to survive. Lying is terrific and getting rid of the enemy is not evil."

Augie fired the innocent mechanic, who violently threatened his life as Brio chased him with a wrench. Victor almost laughed out loud. Then Augie drove Victor home and confessed how it really was.

"I make a living in the shop and donate the rest of my life as a public servant."

"Huh?"

"I'm undercover, of course. I'm a volunteer narc."

"You're kidding! Wow!"

"*You* thought I'm one dumb guy, right? You want in, Victor?"

Victor listened.

"We need info on the kids hanging around the Mall. Plenty of drugs there. We're not sure who's supplying."

"I'll help you."

"You'd be an informer?" Augie asked suspiciously. "You wouldn't mind?"

"Oh, I mind plenty. A squealer like me is definitely a scumbag, but I got my reasons."

Brio shook his head. "You better explain 'em, kid."

"My brother Felipe is in with Lopez these days."

"Bad news!" Brio looked solemn.

"Right. But Felipe just started. He's tossing money around like discount coupons. Before he does something for jail time, I want him busted, the dumb fuck!"

"You help me good, and if your brother's just another bagman, he'll get a suspended sentence."

"That so?"

"Fuckin' A."

VICTOR

After they shook hands on it, Victor tossed in a little perq. "I can help you with the car break-ins at the Mall parking lot."

Brio smiled like a shark. Victor felt sick, even faint. "Kid, you're a find!"

"Just this time," Victor repeated, and looking away from Brio, continued squealing.

The local paper carried the news as front-page headlines for a week; there were more than fifty arrests. Angel Lopez had been shot, was still in critical condition. Felipe's name was never mentioned. Some cops had kicked the shit out of him, tore his new duds, and dumped him in the hallway of the Cruzes' apartment house. The following day, Felipe began painfully taking out the garbage. José was even more slowly reading a gourmet cookbook. When Victor returned from the body shop, his brothers prevented him from going into the bedroom until after supper.

With a grunting flourish, Felipe opened a bottle of cheap French red wine.

"It's a great year, bro," José lied. José had baked blueberry muffins and chicken basted with orange juice. Side dishes were raw broccoli and Cape Cod potato chips. Most of the chicken parts, muffins, and vegetables were dumped on Victor's plate. Victor was too weary to think much, except to eat all that was offered.

Felipe, moaning slightly from his sore ribs, said, "While the cops were working me over, one of 'em said I had a good friend looking out for me."

José's handsome face lit up in pleasure and excitement. "You did it, Victor! You saved that goon's ass."

"It was Poppa's idea," Victor lied, embarrassed.

"Just thanks, Victor, thanks," Felipe said, and began eating with his hands again.

José ignored Felipe's brutish manners and smiled at Victor like he was hypnotized. Victor just kept eating.

VICTOR

After Felipe and José put away the dishes and cleaned up the kitchen, they formally led Victor into the master bedroom. The dim lamp light had been replaced by a glaring bulb; it was almost a spotlight.

There were new sheets on the bed, matching pillowcases for the new foamy pillows, and two new blankets. The bed looked like a goddamned commercial.

"After all these months, we're still together. That is a miracle," José sighed.

"So is not being in the Bronx or the lock-up," confessed Felipe.

For the ghost of Raymondo Cruz, touching the sheets and squeezing the bed, it was a supremely proud moment. Here was José in apron and house slippers fussing over a hot meal; Felipe, battered, but still not in handcuffs; and Victor, at nineteen, with the lowest I.Q. of the three, becoming stronger and wiser every waking moment. Tactfully, the brothers left Victor alone. Raymondo Cruz lay curled at the end of the bed like a pet dog, while Victor lay back and began playing with himself. Soon his erection was a pole stretching to the ceiling. He was Victor Cruz, the man, the true provider.

Felicia

By now, Victor recognized that the mere slump of Raymondo Cruz's shoulders, the bending of his wrinkled lime-green slacks, and the downcast shabby skinny face signified nothing tragic. Odds were high Poppa was only meditating, for no tears slid around. Victor was correct, for the wan ghost was happily thinking what a good life his sons were hammering and fumbling out. Raymondo was very relieved his Cruzes were not girl-crazy. Even now, without watchdog nuns and social worker informers from the Sacred Home, despite tasting the complete freedom of an apartment, the three boys rarely entertained girls and gave few parties.

Only José had the genuine interest in all girls and women, but Felipe and Victor wisely held their horny loving impulses in tight rein and under CIA-intensity scrutiny. Early sexual jousts had been brutal, hurried moments against the walls of Sacred Home's cavernous locker room. Twice Victor had been accused of rape, but who could believe local teenaged girls known to wrap their legs around a boy's shoulders and yip like a dog.

"Perhaps all sex is rape," Raymondo whispered to Victor, who passed on such wisdom to his two brothers. And José would usually scribble down any of Poppa's sayings into an old lined notebook.

"Oh my son, life is a highway filled with potholes. Without women you have less holes to ruin you." Victor tried to pass off this line as his own, but José sensed its true spokesman and finally Victor admitted it was not his style.

Felipe grunted in a mumbling voice, "Ah, our old man is nothing to write about in a damn notebook."

"You're dumb," José snapped.

"About him you're dumber," Felipe challenged. "Poppa's no damn hero. He never did nothing but get gunned down trying to rob a fucking bank with a shitty water gun."

"So what, asshole, our father died for us. He wasn't selfish, you jerk—for us he died."

"Christ, to aim a water gun at a bank guard is nuts."

José began to shake in anger. "You dare mock him, you gorilla!"

Felipe blew cigar smoke into the kid's face. "Cool it, little man. I just don't remember him and you don't either."

Victor saw José was thinking of hitting Felipe with a chair and stepped between them. "José, here's a fiver. Get us some Chicken Delightful. You hear me, José?"

Victor just stared and stared at the folded note that had been stuck under the door. Finally, he opened it and sighed deeply.

FELICIA

Dear Victor Cruz,
  I see you every day going to work. You are a responsible, handsome boy. I live nearby. If you wish to answer, leave a note in your mailbox and write Felicia on the envelope.

Victor tossed the note away and didn't consider answering. He had noticed a sweet-faced, extremely fat young girl watching him, guessed it was she sending all the notes. Who needs a fatty who always smiles? Once she's in your apartment, she probably never stops yelling. Victor never met her gaze, nor did he answer any of the bi-weekly notes she left.

Dear Victor,
  We are brothers and sisters in feelings. I know it. I feel it and I'm certain. I saw you in the Mall. We are one, won't you smile at me or answer or even write over this note? I am Felicia.
  I love you.

Dear Felipe,
  You are big and strong, so much bigger than your brothers. Are you sweet as you are powerful? One of my girlfriends said she saw you take apart a loudmouth drunk at the Topless Palace. I know you are a good man. Send my love to your brothers.

Felipe was excited by the letter, but he was leery of the writer, of anyone who could write. It was easier to try a quickie with the topless girls who were very friendly after the show was over. Sometimes they did everything free, if you walked them to the bus stop and waited in the freezing night until the last city bus showed up.

43

FELICIA

Dear José,

  You are the youngest and the most handsome and you always smile. I think you even smiled at me once. Do you remember? It was in Sears. I touched your shoulder as you were putting a hammer inside your coat and you jerked back and smiled. I dream about your smile. I feel a little like your mother, but not really, only sometimes. I am a day-shift telephone operator. I have wanted to call you, but you have no phone. You must be lonely, too.

José curtly answered Felicia's letter and invited her over. She quickly replied: Yeah, sure, thanks.

José prepared for his date the usual way: he took a shower, covered himself with baby lotion and Felipe's virile cologne; he wore no underwear or t-shirt, selected very tight slacks and a polo that crushed his small rib cage. José knew he looked and acted sexier without underwear. Walking around in a scuffy pair of dirty, fake-fur slippers, José, only five feet tall, looked like an ill child or worried lover.

The ghost of Raymondo Cruz loitered in the empty bathroom and confessed, "José is my favorite. He has the spirit; he seeks and embraces life. Woe to him!" So he didn't squeal to Victor, who planned to go to the movies with Felipe, that Felicia was invited over tonight. Then Raymondo cut out.

Felicia knocked meekly, three times. José opened the door and bowed formally. Felicia giggled, and he flashed his great smile. Felicia had brought two meatball heroes, a six-pack, and one large ginger ale.

"I think the heroes are still hot," she said.

Wow, she was fat; Victor was right. And she was black as racists' bad dreams. He was very anxious to have her naked. Victor and Felipe would be gone at

FELICIA

least two hours, but you never know. José's immediate erection threatened to pierce his cheaply constructed zipper. Felicia saw and looked away after a while, so José took heart and her hand.

"Look, uh, Felicia, could we eat later?"
"Sure."
"What I want now is to do something else. Ok?"
"You wrote me a nice letter. I keep it in my purse."
"I can't spell good."
"That didn't matter. It had feeling, really."
"You still in high school, huh?"
She nodded.
"I think I saw you in a class once."
"You ever go to my school?"
"Nah. I got thrown out of the Home last year, but I walk around your high school sometimes."
"Really?"
"I can't read or write."
"It was a beautiful letter, José."
"Bullshit."
She took his hand. "I can teach you a little if you want. I'd love to be a teacher, but my marks are no good."
"Where do you live?"
"Next block. The big house near the old railroad station."
"In that big house!"
"We live on the second floor—me, my mother, and two little sisters. My brothers are in the Army."
"Exploited," Jose orated.
"No, they like it."
"You got a nice high school."
"Yeah, but nothing changes, except you boys living here."

He lost his erection during the last few minutes, and he was surprised. Usually without underwear his thing was sensitive as hell, jumping up and around like a damn rabbit.

"You want to see Victor's room?"

"Ok."

"He's got the good bedroom. See, he does most of the work."

"Oh."

José pushed open the door; the bed was neat as a pin.

She said, "Nice color you boys colored, I mean painted, the room."

"Yeah, you like pink?"

"It's very bright."

"Hot colors," he said, taking his hand and nervously squeezing the tip of a sleeping cock.

Felicia was looking only at him.

"I can't wake it up; you wanna try?"

"You want me to?"

"Yeah, then we can eat the heroes."

She unzipped him.

"I didn't know whether you like soda or beer."

"We got wine."

"Oh, I could've brought that too."

She had drawn him out over his pants. Felicia was not squeezing, only patting. He dropped his pants, pulled away gently, and jumped on the bed. She followed and the damn bed split—broke as if chopped in half by a master woodcutter.

"Oh God," she cried. Her baby-fat thighs rolled to his pinching. He pulled down her pants, tossing her massive frilly bikini across the room.

Felicia said, "Oh, are you going to be in trouble? The bed is really busted."

FELICIA

"We can fix the bed later. It's always breaking," he lied politely. She was really black and smelled like sugar. Her breasts cascaded into his arms and he gulped one at a time. Finally he crawled inside. She rested, sighed a lot, and waited for him to finish.

"Can I still stay and eat here?" José patted her all over, but she cried louder and louder.

"I'm an easy lay," she whispered, "since I was very young."

She touched a pimple on her chin.

"Really, you can tell me to go away."

"I'd like to have supper with you, Felicia."

She said primly, "I'll get dressed and heat up the stuff. You try and fix the bed."

When Raymondo, Felipe, and Victor returned, Felicia was sitting on the worn small couch watching the TV news. José had saved a can of beer for each brother. They did not look happy, but Felicia smiled warmly. Victor sniffed the room.

"It looks cleaner," he said.

Felicia shrugged, "I dusted a little."

Victor grimaced, "It is cleaner."

Felipe asked, "Any more beer?"

Felicia said, "Next time I'll bring more."

José was nervous. The bed was not really fixed. It looked ok, but if a cockroach crept by, the foundation would collapse. And the bed was all that Victor loved. Felicia lifted her bosom as if to say hello and wriggled her big ass along the couch. God, José hoped *that* didn't collapse. Victor still looked for a lone dust ball, but failed to find one.

She spoke again, "Really nice place." José felt tiny—

everyone in the small apartment was much bigger than him anyway—but tonight, right now, they seemed giants.

Felicia said to Victor, "I really love your bedroom."

"You wanna see it again with me?" Felipe joked.

"Gladly." She offered her arm, but Felipe grabbed a buttock. Moments later there was a tremendous sound of something irrevocably broken followed by silence, some coughing, and then much laughing, with occasional thuds. Felipe came out in his underwear, wiping his lips with the back of a hairy hand.

He said to Victor, "Gravy train, if you don't mind splinters. We'll fix it up tomorrow."

The ghost of Raymondo Cruz followed Victor to the bedroom door.

"Be certain she is protected either by pill or something else."

"Don't worry, Pop, I've been around. I got something in my wallet for emergencies."

Felicia lurked somewhere in the room. It was very dark. Finally he saw an even darker blob.

He called out, "Hey, you on the pill?"

"Every day," she replied softly.

"Go my son," Raymondo Cruz smiled awkwardly.

"José, José" someone was calling, but José was forcing himself into the deep sleep of the weary and lost. He willed not to awaken until late in the morning.

Dear José,
 I did it for you. Your brothers were angry when they saw me. Your ass would have been broken when they found the bed. So I did it with the big one first. Now

FELICIA

they know nothing. Don't be angry. I would do it again for you. I will do it again for you. Only see it's my love that does it. Also see how much better I write than I talk. That's from school. I'll get you books. Maybe you can even come to my class sometimes. Don't be mad, José.

You are the only one who cares what he does and how he does it to a girl. You're small, but very good. I bet you could break any fine bed.

Please answer. We can meet other places I know and remember about the high school. I love only you.

Felicia

José had not saved any of her previous notes. Tears came to his eyes as he destroyed this note, too.

Raymondo Cruz forgot his status, forgot the imbalance of life and death, and shouted out, "Oh love is beautiful—sad and demeaning and yet very beautiful."

Raymondo, the concerned parent, whispered to Victor that evening, "Remember to tell José."

"Of course, Poppa."

"Say it exactly as I do: love is beautiful, but sad and demeaning and yet very beautiful."

Dutifully, Victor then repeated it many times before he got it exactly right.

Momma

It was good there was no phone in the Cruz apartment. The brothers always dialed a pay phone without hope and in some fear and bewilderment. They had no basic telephone manners, never saying a hello or goodbye, and only screaming their questions and answers into the receiver, sure that only the power of their voices could get through to the listener. In fact, had they now possessed such a marvel, it might be the end of achievement, for the phone was surely the last step forward, almost like finishing high school or attending community college. A sufficient miracle was their own mailbox, usually filled with junk circulars and nothing of personal communication, except bills. Though nothing exciting had yet arrived, no nun was peeking under an envelope flap either. CRUZ had been beautifully scribbled onto a white card taped to the top of the mailbox.

Victor would ask, "Hey, any mail?" José and Felipe would stir, become a little animated, and both would usually volunteer to go downstairs and check it out. Victor usually joined them to look and see.

The ghost of Raymondo Cruz trembled with fear when he saw and smelled the letter Victor held aloft like some prize booty.

"It smells funny," Victor admitted. Poppa was acting funny as hell the past few months, but today he was shaking like a sick fish at the end of a long, cruel hook. Victor seriously wondered if a ghost could get sick. But knowing Poppa's poor luck, it could happen.

"Burn the letter and wash your hands in strong detergent."

"Huh?"

"I rarely ask you to obey me, but listen carefully, my son. Burn the letter! You have a poor memory anyway; forget it ever arrived."

"Hey, but it's airmail from New York."

"Burn it, wash your hands in detergent three times a day for seven days."

Too much. The old man was maybe sick and definitely senile.

"Christ, a letter can't hurt. It ain't from the cops or the government."

"Worse. It's from your Momma."

"How can you tell? She never wrote before."

"This letter is from my wife and your Momma. The envelope bears her stench and evil fumes."

"Maybe, maybe, but I'm going to open it. We never get mail anyway. I'm not throwing it away."

Raymondo Cruz sadly hung his head, sighed very softly, and left.

Cautiously the three brothers circled the letter. José, very excited and scared, stuttered slightly, "If-f-f he told-d-d you to toss it away, you should-d-da done it-t-t."

"You speak like the baby you are," Victor spat.
"Yeah, pipe down," added Felipe.
Red crayon printed on loose-leaf . . .

   You better come damn fast, all of you, not just my josé, estrella will help she got a car   victor get a shovel we'll use your backyard come damn fast you hear
                                           Momma.

Felipe was the first to speak. "We're a week late already."
"A week is not late for her. Anyway, I'd rather see Momma anytime than Estrella. *She's* the fucking witch."
"Yeah, Victor, Momma isn't like Estrella unless she has a fit."
José spoke softly, "There's plenty wrong. Someone died, right?"
Felipe, resembling a wise Buddha, nodded, "Maybe one of her watch dogs kicked the bucket and she wants mourners."
Only Victor grinned.
The ghost of Raymondo Cruz loitered in the bathroom retching dry heaves—That woman is evil, oh, she is the devil, especially her eyes and smile.

The boys' hearts sagged when Estrella opened the apartment door. After a week, they figured Estrella would be back hustling at the social club. But she had waited for them. She wore a white blouse and black skirt, a man's ill-fitting tweed sports coat, an applejack cap, and Converse sneakers. For a second, the older boys lost hope and would have fled, but José raced in, eager to see Momma.

"You goddamn kids are late."

"We just got the letter. We don't live at the Home anymore."

Estrella had aged. The Cruzes happily noted that the gypsy was now dumpy and less savage-looking. Her voice had deteriorated like a slowed-down 45.

The boys almost giggled and lost most of their fear.

They were ready to begin mocking. Surely Estrella was one hustler whose price had gone down though there was an inflation.

"Who died?" José asked.

"This child is one of us!" Estrella screeched. "He senses things. Ah, he knows. I'll get Maria." She ran off.

José snapped his fingers. "It's the damn baby. Remember I told you how it was sick the last time I visited."

"One of her damn dogs ate it. Thought the baby'd crawl off with the TV," Felipe guffawed.

Victor said, "You're right, Felipe. I bet you're right."

José, ever Momma's boy, whispered, "She probably banged it around, but it *was* sick."

"Who's the father of that kid? She know, José?"

"A TV repairman."

"Just say you don't know, wise ass."

"It's the fucking truth. Some guy was living there, walking around like a big-shot doctor with a satchel full of picture tubes, fixing her sets."

Maria came in the room surrounded by her pack of attack dogs. The animals had just been fed and were not snapping or surly. They seemed almost pets and perfect hosts. Momma wore her usual gown, the white frilly old-fashioned party dress she was married in and had worn at her husband's funeral.

MOMMA

Maria Cruz had aged better than her friend. Even her worst features, her teeth—sharp, yellow corn niblets—could make a man think erotically. José thought Momma looked very beautiful in her gown, and Victor and Felipe reluctantly agreed.

"It is the baby. You're right, my José."

"Don't worry, boys, we threw the father out. His cock is polluted to give Maria such a runt."

Maria began to sob.

Estrella chanted. "Yes, yes, and she loved this baby. she was ready to be a mother, a momma to this one. She had the experience to make this child grow big and strong, and the baby dies on her."

Momma was really bawling. The dogs were getting nervous, ready to jump the sons. Who could ever remember a time when not one of the fourteen TVs was on? Truly an occasion of mourning!

"So we have waited for you to come and bury this special child," Estrella announced.

Momma finished crying. She held her gown close as if it were a quilt. José would have done anything for her. He saw how Poppa could have tried a bank.

"We'll bury it in your back yard. Estrella has a car."

"What back yard? We live in an apartment house."

"In the country there are *apartment houses* too? Oh, Estrella, there is no hope. I'll put my Bernardo in the garbage."

"We go to the country anyway and there we'll give this child a proper funeral. He's rotted here a week. Bernardo must be buried with honor." Felipe couldn't help laughing at how the gypsy spoke.

Momma said, "Come look at the child." In the back room amidst obsolete TVs and tubes was a vinyl suitcase. The smell emitting from the piece of luggage was worse than the animal excrement in every room. Other children ran by, but the boys ignored these kids as if they were flies.

"Where can we go, Victor?" Momma whispered.

"To the Home, to Sacred Home, and bury it in the woods."

"The Home where you lived?"

"You was never there, Momma. But it's very pretty. Really country."

Estrella put on her cape. "I'll warm up the car."

Estrella's Chevy had no muffler and no shocks, so it was a noisy, bumpy ride back to the country. Momma wouldn't let go of the suitcase and the boys felt they had never left the Bronx, but finally they were out in fresh air. Estrella parked off the main road, while the boys pushed back wild growth that hid a short-cut behind the recreation hall.

"We had dances there."

Momma nodded.

Raymondo Cruz had followed his sons past the Jersey border as far as the George Washington Bridge, and now he sat upon a tollbooth awaiting their return. He trembled violently the moment he spied his wife and Estrella. Despite a choking spasm and the furious pain of bullets assaulting his body once again, Raymondo pursued the car.

Under the cool star-cluttered sky, Momma stumbled several times in her bedroom slippers but would accept no help. They walked silently in single file along the dark narrow path. Victor led the way. Momma, Estrella, José, and Felipe in the rear, and the ghost of Raymondo Cruz followed overhead.

"The shovel! Shit, we didn't take the shovel!" Victor cried out.

"Leave it here, leave the damn suitcase here. Nobody comes around," José said.

"What if we get caught?" Victor blurted.

"Never, never!" Momma screamed.

"We came here," Estrella pointed out. "Others will come too. The child must be buried now or he will walk the face of the moon at night, clawing down at us, seeking our souls."

Momma fainted.

Victor shouted, "You're a bugged out gypsy. Knock it off!"

"Look, look!"

Momma lay face down. "I won't leave until Bernardo is under ground, not pestered by buses or subways. He always slept poorly. Give me my suitcase."

Estrella quacked, "It is a miracle." The shabby suitcase was levitating slowly into the sky.

The ghost of Raymondo Cruz was cradling the suitcase and singing, "Don't worry, little one. You'll be safe soon. We'll fly upstate away from all of them. Sleep, little one."

Momma cried, "A miracle! My first miracle!"

Victor agreed. It must be Poppa saving the day, but he couldn't see him. This *was* a special bit.

"God has spoken, Maria. He is taking Bernardo to heaven. Let's go back to the Bronx."

Estrella offered the brothers a ride, but Victor didn't wish the women to know where they lived.

"We'll camp out tonight."

Momma tried, "Give me money for the bridge."

"We need gas," Estrella said.

Victor gave them two dollars, and the car sputtered off into the night.

When Poppa returned in a new black suit, Victor saluted him snappily. Poppa smiled affectionately.

Victor called out, "I got to go to work, Poppa. We'll talk another time."

"Of course, my son. Work hard, think of today only."

But Victor already knew that wisdom was learning to concentrate on the minutes you *live,* not *have* lived or *may* live. That sounded like something Poppa might have asked to be passed on to Felipe and José. To honor Raymondo Cruz, Victor washed his hands in detergent three times a day, but for only three days. However, the point and tribute were not lost on his Poppa.

Sweet Saturday

"This damn tape recorder better be working perfect. José found it in the garbage up the street and checked it out. He said the rich always toss out good stuff to buy newer, freshly advertised merchandise. I just don't want to waste my time talking.

"You're supposed to feel better off, you know, relieved after telling someone else your troubles; maybe, but I don't want to deal with any shifty priest. Outside my brothers I got no one to trust, so having this machine hear my shit is fine. But this machine gotta keep its trap shut unless I pull the plug and press the button.

"Look, I know we're never going to be safe and sound, but it's Saturday morning and, hey, I just paid the rent, so everything is cool for a few weeks. Our landlord, Andy Kousitsky, is from another world, a hundred years ago—he's got a stringy beard, watery eyes, a long hairy crooked nose and crooked green teeth. He always wears this moldy black coat that hangs to the ground and he's got a green velvet cowboy hat with ear flaps. And I like it when Kousitsky keeps telling me we're good tenants.

"We live on the second floor. On the first floor is an empty luncheonette. Third floor is empty too because heat can't get up that high and some important pipes don't reach that far, either. This used to be a helluva busy street until our landlord got suckered out when the highway department built an extension to the superhighway a block away and poof goes any sort of traffic. The dumb Russians Kousitsky tricked into renting the luncheonette couldn't make it work. They gave up quick once they didn't see a car or bus for a week. Kousitsky says they broke a five-year lease. He ain't going to put them in jail, but he won't do 'em any more favors.

"Hey, I'm not blind either. I know this old town is falling flat on its mushy face. Urban renewal could begin here tonight, but don't worry, all the whites who have always lived here, they don't care shit about progress. They don't mind Main Street creaking and cracking and all the old homes rotting and leaning down like they're hunchbacked, because man, if that means no newcomers come around to live and make trouble, then let it all fall down. They don't even hate us much anymore, since we don't have parties except on weekends and holidays, and we'd never rip off a neighbor. They even say 'How ya doin'.

"Town people are very clean, pretty old, and tough, and they worry only about local things. They already lost all their elm trees fifteen years ago. An oak disease is coming, and everyone is shitless about the locusts next summer. Committees and vigilante groups are around curing oak trees and planning to demolish locusts. One thing nobody worries about is being

SWEET SATURDAY

mugged. So what if the town is creaking and the houses are dying faster than the owners, this is still a dumb, gentle place.

"Of course right outside town we got everything—a huge bowling alley, a drive-in movie that only shows X flicks, McDonalds, six or seven bars, many pizza joints, and three custard stands. Ok, ok, little machine, that's it for now. Everybody's getting up!"

Felicia had already dropped in. Soon she was swept up in the air of excitement and promised to make them take-out lunches Monday. One true fact about Felicia was that she never lied or just talked. She always came across, though she had the big eyes only for José.

"The apartment looks real good."

Victor nodded grumpily. "It always looks ok."

"But it seems sunnier and cleaner."

José giggled. "Who knows. But you better dust anyway."

Like a very heavy, but not ungraceful, butterfly she pranced from room to room with her dust mop.

Felipe belched a couple of times and said, "She looks like a cartoon."

José said defensively, "And you look like a convicted axe murderer."

Victor warned, "It's going to be hot today. So don't act like monkeys. Cut it out."

"I don't wanna go out this morning, Felicia," José shouted, though she was only a few feet away.

"Oh why not? José, you promised!"

Felipe groaned. "Oh, don't break the lady's heart, punk."

Victor promised, "We'll figure out something to do."

José, annoyed, pointed out, "That's a big problem of yours, Victor. You always gotta keep busy. Why not just lay around?"

Victor, sorry now he'd not let Felipe move in on José, sternly said, "This ain't the beach. Why you so damn lazy?"

José smiled sweetly, "I can't hear you, big brother. I'm planning my Saturday vacation right here."

Felipe asked, "José, you don't paint anymore?"

"Right!"

"How come? It's easy bucks."

"Simple, fool. I lost my talent. If I find it again, I'll be the first to tell you."

Felicia laughed.

Felipe gave her a filthy look. "You gotta be a lousy dishwasher again." And he assumed a Hulk Hogan stance.

Felicia kissed José good-bye and waved to the other brothers.

"I gotta go, but I may be back later with a friend."

"As long as she doesn't look like you."

Felipe grinned.

Victor apologized, "Ignore him. He thinks he's Eddie Murphy these days."

But Felicia, insulted, stormed out. José ran to the landing, "If you don't come back, remember lunch for Monday!"

Rudolfo Rivera knocked at the door. A Sacred Home graduate, Rudy was sullenly tolerated at the Cruz apartment. His parents had died in a car accident. Relatives in San Juan never stopped sending money and clothes, so he'd never been truly abandoned and lorded his privileged position over the other battered orphans.

SWEET SATURDAY

Right now Rudy was living off a waitress, Gloria Simoski, a former lesbian, now straight and interested only in cocks under twenty. Usually he came with grass or food, so their hostility was slow in erupting, but no one really liked Rudolfo, who, despite his advantages, was weird as hell. He kept a coffin in Gloria's apartment and would screw the waitress in it. He often napped in the unlined coffin. The Cruzes vividly remembered the bully's vicious torture tricks on puppies and kittens, but they didn't fear or feel sorry for him.

"Hey, Rudolfo, what's happening?"

"Rudy, what you bring?"

"A basketball."

"You didn't bring your coffin?" José asked.

"No, wise guy, it stays home like your teddy bear."

By now José had seen plenty of roaches; though he hadn't heard them talk, he had stopped killing them. But many people talked like a roach. They walked slow, glum, and without hope, ready for someone to stomp out their pathetic lives. Rudolfo was one guy who was clearly a sick roach. Another definite roach was the slimy manager of the Grand Union where José pulled most of his rip-offs. He recalled Estrella's warning, "Don't mess with a roach," and kept his hands and feet to himself.

"You say something, José?" Felipe asked.

Rudolfo acted wise. "Hey, José, fix the contrast, will ya?"

But José didn't answer and wouldn't move a quarter of an inch for any Rudy Rivera.

After a six-pack, Felipe became surlier and figured José looked like a damn pygmy. "You're souped up, man."

José paid him no mind.

"Hah," Felipe doggedly slurred, "Remember at the

Sacred Home when you was fourteen and pimping for the senior girls?"

"I'm seventeen now and that's over."

"You think I'm so goddamned dumb I don't know how old you are?"

"What's your point, Felipe? Do you remember?"

Felipe raised his fist. José ducked, though no punch was thrown, and Victor warned, "It's only Saturday morning, not even Saturday night yet. Stay cool."

Felipe spat out, "Yeah, José, I remember my point. Now you walk like some Puerto Rican big shot, but then you were selling pussy like grapes off a tree."

"Shithead, I don't deny I exploited, but *no* more! I stopped forever. Malcolm X was once a pimp."

"You say the same dumb fucking thing every day!"

"I'll keep saying it until you understand it, retarded gorilla."

"You got a fresh mouth, José," Victor cautioned.

"I don't want to hit you or you might be exploited in two." Felipe roared with laughter. Rudolfo giggled like the fag he was and the crisis passed.

"Since you didn't bring no food, Rudy, let's play us some ball."

The slit of land angled between a state highway and the town's official boundary line was a no-man's property, gifted to the village. The Department of Public Works hastily set up two benches, three swings, a black-topped square with a cement-bedded pole, warped backboard, and a ridiculous steel-mesh net, and dubbed what they had done a playground. The sun was forever shielded by the smog of exhaust fumes; tin cans and paper littered the bumpy grounds. With the arrival of the Cruzes and Rudolfo, more kids magically appeared. It was as if the other boys in the neighborhood peered out their windows awaiting some sucker to come and ruin his ball.

The Cruzes always played as a team; they enjoyed being with each other and competing against others. Felipe stood in the pivot while José and Victor ran past him like frightened waterbugs. They laughed and spun the ball away from their opponents' grasps. This laughter was not taunting or disparaging, merely a delighted laughter of the innocent, like a little kid whipping out his wiener and peeing in the flowers, astonished by his power and bravado and the nice feeling the wind made nudging his pecker. The Cruzes played as if drilled by a martinet. At times they forgot to shoot the ball in the basket. They never raised their voices in anger and sweated marvelous beads that tasted like bittersweet soda. They glided among the taller boys, guarding them, finally remembering the rules of the game, and scored easy basket after basket.

"Enough," Rudy Rivera announced grimly, "it's over. You guys are too damn much."

Felicia and her cousin Myra sat on the front steps. Felicia, in trying to snare José's full attention, had gone on a strict Weight Watcher's diet and lost fifty pounds. Now hungry all the time, she dreamed of junk food; in the mornings she lamented her rigid discipline.

Her cousin wanted to take off. "C'mon, Felicia, they're not here. Let's go."

She soothed Myra, "Be patient, I got a key."

Felicia loved coming to the Cruz apartment. Sometimes it was enough to wait and not even see the brothers. Being inside their tiny place was like a recess from life. An hour later, when the boys returned sweaty and

SWEET SATURDAY

happy, Myra and Felicia were sitting on the couch. The apartment was hot and stuffy. A breeze snuck in, banging the window shades. Felicia introduced her cousin. "This is Myra from Charlotte, North Carolina."

"Terrific."

"Hey, she ever smile?"

"When somebody says something funny."

Rudy Rivera flashed a mean, bored look at the girls, as the Cruzes took turns palming the scruffy basketball. The two girls ignored him, but Rudy had nowhere else to go. Desperately, he tossed a twenty-dollar bill on the floor; now he had everyone's attention. But no one fought to grab the bill.

"What's up, Rudy?" Victor asked.

"I'd like to make it with all of you. You can split the twenty."

Felicia asked if he was kidding. Shy Myra still was not smiling or talking.

"He's not kidding," José said. "He's a pervert who wants to be king of the mountain."

Felipe covered the bill with a ripped Converse. "Only a twenty, Rudy? Aren't our asses worth more than twenty?"

Rudolfo said, "I don't have any more. Look, everything goes. I'm down for anything."

Victor half smiled, "You don't want to fuck around. You want to drown us like you did the cats and pull out our eyes like you did to the Home dogs."

Felipe waved two fists like high-flying flags.

"Beat it," José advised.

Victor opened the door and said, "Thanks for the twenty, stupid."

Felipe shoved Rudy toward the open door. Rudy accepted the hint and took off.

SWEET SATURDAY

While the boys showered, Felicia and Myra cleaned up. "What do you want to do with his basketball?"

Victor, covered by shabby towels, answered happily, "Keep it. Rudy'll show again. This happens every month. He's a real crazy and we're his only friends. He'll be back, maybe with his coffin."

Victor handed the twenty to Felicia. "You and Myra get plenty of chicken and a couple of six-packs and dessert. Save some dough for a taxi after you load up." Felicia and Myra returned with dozens of greasy, gray, broken chicken parts, sweet watery cole slaw, lousy potato salad, icy beer, piss-warm soda, and melted spumoni. They all laughed, belched, farted, licked the soft chicken bones, choked, and laughed some more. Now Myra did nothing but giggle and giggle. She had real big jagged teeth.

"Can we sleep here tonight?" Felicia meekly asked.

"Sure," Victor replied.

Each boy politely waited his turn to fuck each girl; though it was lively there was no cursing and it was almost a solemn religious occasion. Afterward they took showers until the hot water ran out.

Felipe called out, "Hey Victor, is it Monday yet?"

"No, plenty of time."

Someone giggled and someone else whispered, "*Good, good.*"

The Word

Lately, José was trying to figure out better ways to shape his future. Perplexed by this sudden maturity, he slept poorly, squinted a lot, and half-heartedly and sadly took a second part-time job.

In the past three months, José's handsome face had fleshed out, become softer and puffier; worry pouches had settled in under his cloudy gray eyes. José was now far less lively, often taciturn, even grimly introspective. But one humid evening over tepid pizza and chilly beer, he became animated once more as he loudly philosophized.

"Wow, even eating tonight with our own fingers in our own joint without any watchdogs around is still fuckin' amazing. I mean it. Lots has happened. Man, it could be a movie."

Felipe said, "Jerk, it's not over. How can it be a movie?"

"A movie is over when it's over. You can make it end anytime. Christ."

"A book too," Victor butted in.

Felipe muttered, "How do you know. We don't read books."

"Everybody knows it. Knock it off, Felipe."

"We never even had an album," José softly reminisced.

"Huh. Shit, José, you are nuts. We got plenty of records."

"But no pictures, snapshots. Photo albums to look over and remember."

"Jeez, remember what? You wanna see your baby pictures?"

"No, I want to see yours, though. Felipe, you had to be the ugliest baby that ever fell on its face."

Victor pointed out, "There were no cameras in the Bronx."

"Aah, you guys are crazy. What's to remember."

"Knock it off, Felipe," Victor cautioned.

Felipe ignored him. "What's to read, what's to see? You wanna stay up all night having nightmares?"

José shouted, "We need scrapbooks, and Victor's right too—we should be in a book. We'd make a great story. And I could star in the movie. You could sell tickets for it, Felipe! Be an usher!"

"Bullshit," Felipe banged his fists on the rickety coffee table. "Bullshit."

That night Poppa watched Victor toss restlessly in bed. Finally Victor, lifting his sweaty head from the sour and battered pillow, sat up and groaned. Poppa offered him a towel to dry off. "Was Felipe right, Victor? Are you having nightmares?"

"Felipe is a moron. Somebody ought to write us up. Only you know our history, Poppa."

The ghost shook his head, "All of you are my story. You must tell it."

"Damn, Poppa, how?"

THE WORD

Poppa didn't know either. José once seemed the natural story teller, but now working two part-time jobs and saving money to cheaply buy an American dream made him silent too.

"José will not do?" Poppa asked.

"Right. And Felipe needs brain surgery to even read or write."

Poppa pointed to Victor, who tried to go to sleep but couldn't.

Poppa whispered loudly, "Without a past you walk around mumbling like a vegetable or a junkie."

"You think I could do it? The damn tape recorder is busted."

"History is an important subject. You must write it, then!"

"First I gotta get some sleep. Shit."

"Any beginning is important." Poppa advised all night.

Victor was surprised that José and Felipe didn't mock his plodding earnestness, and more astounding was the army of words that marched to his brisk command. And if Victor's thoughts didn't line up in a straight order, so fucking what? He was very fortunate to remember anything. So he scanned newspapers and magazines and tried occasionally to read a dictionary. Poppa tested him on the words like it was a spelling bee. At times Victor felt transformed into a massive fountain spraying salvoes of words, sentences, and paragraphs. And he wrote down his scattered memories fast, barely mentioning the moment Poppa died. Victor darted around recalling parts of a scene and scraps of conversation. And Poppa flew about the room like an agitated bat, cheering his son on, and suggested, "Tell the highlights, Victor. The highlights."

Though beaten regularly, Victor had enjoyed his life at Sacred Home for Fallen Angels. He never forgot how Sacred Home looked when he first arrived. There were clean white buildings scattered over the front lawn. Older graying buildings topped by weird turrets leaned on sloping hills. Below the hills were modern cottages spread-eagling an endless field. The land was deep green and packed with flowers of every color and size. There was a sweet breeze and the sky was a spotless blue. Birds were chirping loudly and flying recklessly overhead. The orphans seemed happy, and there were even sounds of laughter. Church bells were ringing and you couldn't spot too many nuns around. And there were no cops at all. Victor could see a swimming pool and a great many basketball courts in pretty good shape. Victor had wondered if he too, like Poppa, hadn't suddenly died.

Sister Noreen, the head lady for Sacred Home, gave a weekly pep talk. None of her captive audience ever giggled or whispered, but only Victor, the newcomer, raptly listened to her tirades, at least for a while.

"Children, shut up and listen. You have disappointed. Each and every damn one of you. Continually playing with your private parts is going on every day despite the rules and punishments. You will never grow to your full height, realize any of your opportunities, if masturbation continues. It is a highly irreligious, obscene, dirty act. When you reach adulthood you will suffer urinary problems and blockages and your minds will be open sores. Those caught have been denied desserts for a month and all privileges for two months. The punishments, the spot checks, the spying will continue, and we will reward informers. Now stop touching yourselves. Loving oneself is the greatest of sins. You will be punished in the now and the hereafter. Your bodies are not lovely. Now shut up and think about what I have said. And do all your homework."

Once José and Felipe arrived at the Home, Poppa appeared daily urging Victor to watch over his brothers very carefully.

"They are young and frightened of everybody and everything."

"Hey I know, Poppa," Victor said impatiently, "but they'll be ok."

Victor felt Felipe could beat up anybody and wily José could con any dude out of his nuts, if he had to. However, the anxious ghost easily read his eldest son's mind.

"Felipe and José will be in many dumb jams. Woe, woe!"

Victor nodded, "Ok, ok, I'll talk to Manuel Rosado. He'll help us."

At Sacred Home only one kid, Manuel Rosado, dominated. Years ago, Manuel had been left on the steps of a Queens police station. A kind cop dropped the infant off at Sacred Home where Manuel became famous and was such a gracious winner nobody got mad or jealous of his success.

Manuel worked part time at a supermarket and then later at night at a drugstore, besides going full time to high school—so he made extra money and the dean's list. He was the one orphan heading to places like Yale and Princeton. Sister Noreen would pause and speak in a more human, soft voice to him. Some of the younger nuns seemed ready to give him head. He was a saint and also fun to be near. The manager of the supermarket trusted him at the cash register; the pharmacist never doubted that Manuel wouldn't snatch even an aspirin; and the principal was going to frame the acceptance letters from Harvard and Yale and Princeton.

Manuel was never a big shot even when asked for advice. He listened as Victor revealed his brothers' potential for getting into bad trouble. Manuel smiled, "Teach Felipe and José to be clever cowards." Patiently Victor waited for Manuel to continue, since Rosado pep talks were far more on the money than Sister Noreen's shrill lectures.

"Victor, Home kids are always on the lam. But we gotta fake we're ready to settle for society's *honest* life, let 'em think they have the whiphand. Forever," said Manuel.

Victor sighed and grunted.

"The air is never free, so pretend Jesus is your pimp and the nuns will let you alone. Victor, your brothers get me nervous. Felipe and José better never get caught showing their real feelings."

"Right," Victor snapped, "fucking right."

Later Manuel became the first folk hero out of Sacred Home, because when he did graduate and act out against society, Manuel broke every window in the Home and made the institution shake like there was a damn earthquake.

Big cheese priests were invited from New Jersey and New York and even Connecticut to attend Manuel's graduation. The high school auditorium was packed with straight parents from nearby development homes and the pink-cheeked nuns with their holy guests. Hell, Manuel was the first kid from Sacred Home to go to college, and what a college—Yale! Not even white kids in the graduating class were taken by those kinds of colleges. When he walked up to get his diploma, scholarship, and a pat on the afro, Manuel stopped, threw off his cap and gown, and kept walking—but now he was stark naked. First he peed on the principal, then on the diploma; then he put the sopping wet document on the stage, squatted, and farted on it. Soon he was lugged off by a couple of gym teachers. Howling men and women stood up, a unified, screaming lynch mob. Sister Noreen passed out. One of the big-shot priests vomited. Those orphans attending gave Manuel a standing ovation, and they, too, were dragged from the auditorium. Manuel was defined as nuts for a while, shoved into an isolation unit, then let out—and did finally go to Yale. The college people watched him carefully, but he played it cool. He was waiting, and if the right time came again, the right potential, he would attack again. Manuel was lucky, was still lucky; he had his cake, he ate his cake, threw it up, and then got it back.

During Victor's final year at Sacred Home, the sun never stumbled into sight. There was only rotten weather. Winter was the only season. Life just wouldn't stop being bleak and hopeless. No orphan possessed enough sweaters, heavy coats, deeply lined boots, or woolen hats.

Everyone had colds and high fevers. Probably if the brothers had been back in the Bronx they would have had pneumonia at least twice apiece and maybe one of them would have died. Then on a rotten day that seemed like all the others, the sun made a comeback and stayed around for an hour. Next day it stayed longer. After a week it never left the sky. Flowers popped up. The land sighed. Everyone stopped coughing and sneezing. At last the winter was over and the Cruzes and the rest of the Sacred Home orphans were very healthy, very bored, and ready for trouble.

The girl's section of the Home was surrounded by a wire fence topped by barbed wire and guarded twenty-four hours a day by hired pigs—not real cops but more like Santa Clauses out of jobs, though they looked ok when surrounded by snow. They were beefy, red-faced, toothless jerks who chased away the horny kids who tried to sneak through to get at the willing girls. José was starting to get revolutionary ideas and tried to have the dumb guards join them.

"What kind of jobs do you have?" he reasoned. "We should join forces. All oppressed people will be one fist." But the cops just waved him away like he was a stray balloon.

The boys made some plans to sneak past the cops. Sometimes their schemes worked, but many times they failed, until Manuel contributed a master plan. It was a beautiful idea and only the most beautiful looker could make it a success. So Manuel spoke to Consuela. Consuela, who was as free with legs and ass as with her smile, frenched Manuel under a statue facing the Home church. She was delighted with his plan. She loved Manuel because he was so smart; but Consuela was not prejudiced—if you were a Home boy, she'd do it with you, no matter what your looks or I.Q.

Consuela also had a thing for canaries. They kept dying on her, but she kept buying them, and the damn birds kept getting chills or scared to death. There was so much racket in the girls' dorm that one nervous canary committed suicide by beaking itself to death. Consuela would do anything to earn money for more canaries and better cages and warmer covers for the cages. The boys chipped in ten dollars and she agreed to be the siren calling out to the night cop. It was decided to set up the cop at night since evening is best for sneaky fun. And success operates at a better percentage when the stars and moon are around.

People are shocked at simple everyday things, but if

something unbelievable happens, they don't question too much. That was Manuel's premise and it was weird and funny, and many of the orphans didn't understand and thought it wouldn't work. Consuela already had her ten dollars, and so was honor-bound to stroll out clad only in last summer's bikini, holding an empty birdcage, crying she had lost her bird in the laundry room. The cop must follow meekly. Kids were already hiding in the laundry room and would take Polaroids of all the action, blackmail the son-of-a-bitch, and thereby gain entry every night to where pleasure waited and no one would be caught or punished again for simple screwing.

So Consuela guzzled some Dago Red, went out doors, smiled at the guard, who immediately followed her like a lost baby duck. Photographers were on top of the big dryers, snapping the action. Even after Consuela left, the guard still lay on the damp floor looking like an old gray seal. And then, for no reason, the scene got sad. The old guy began humming, also playing with himself—he was that happy. They didn't take any pictures of that, but quietly crept out of the damn place.

It all worked out satisfactorily. But the cop did not exactly understand it was blackmail, for he loved the pictures and kept asking for extras, which he glued to his junky room in the boarding house along the old railroad tracks. And he simply let the boys into the compound because he was in love and understood their desires completely. Strange, but Consuela just paired off with the old cop, and she stayed true to him for the six months more he lived. Then he killed himself. When the boarders broke into the locked room, they found him smelling bad and dead, and all the pictures had been torn off the walls and cooked under the broiler. Only Consuela attended the funeral. She went into deep mourning and completely changed. She did not put out until the next fall—and determined to be a nurse and asked Manuel to help her learn to study, which he did.

And even after Manuel did his own bit at graduation, Consuela continued to do her serious work and she did become a nurse. She is one today at Bellevue. She rarely screws around, since she is too busy being of service to the sick and reading the medical journals. Victor Cruz wrote her that he was doing a patchwork personal history and she wrote back, "The old days sucked." Then he mailed her the part of the history done so far.

She wrote back, "You use the word 'sweet' in the beginning of this history; is 'sweet' your own word? If not, write back and tell me what is your word."

"What does it matter?" Victor wrote back.

She answered, "Love is my word at the Home. I only screwed since it was love for me and, of course, I did love the canaries. Now it is the hospital I love. Manuel took me out for dinner; we went to a fine restaurant. Manuel was wearing a college blazer and turtleneck and is very handsome and still smart. His word is patience, mine is love. You must explain the word to yourself. It is even better than any history. It will make your life clearer if you have one private word. It's better than women or money. You must have this word first before anything. Manuel agrees and sends his best."

Victor wrote back, "My word is sweet and love and patience to you and Manuel."

"Sweet," Victor Cruz added, "is sangria, strawberry ice cream, orange soda, a crowded swimming pool, a good bike, a fat motorcycle, a car that works and has an inspection stamp and is correctly and honestly registered; pants, violet turtlenecks, quality chiba grass,

Adidases, Puerto Rico, seeing Poppa's ghost not too often, getting blown, eating pizza with everything on it with José and Felipe."

"Meditate on sweet," wrote Manuel, "it is only a metaphor, but hang on to the word until it hurts. Have your brothers get words too. Continue the history. You will find other powerful words."

And then Consuela wrote, "I have a patient, an old man who is near death. He has run out of any special words, but we cannot."

Victor Cruz junked his evolving history for a while and lived soberly in the present and warned his brothers to look for the proper word. Each day they came back with new words, new phrases, and they mugged each other with new sounds and ideas. And Victor saw that the history was writing itself. He no longer needed pen or paper.

The Brothers and Mrs. Malloy

PHYSICAL fitness was an essential part of Victor's daily ritual. He did barbell exercises early in the morning and late at night. During the day he left the barbells in the middle of the living room, strongly hinting that his brothers should also participate. But they looked the other way. Occasionally they tripped over the equipment but never lifted it.

As summer drew near, Victor nervously saw how out of shape Felipe and José were. Flab was the great sin and Victor an intense minister who threatened, "Either you work out here, or we go to the park after supper." Felipe and José agreed to the park gig every night, figuring Victor would be tired after building ranch homes. But they were wrong. He was on their tails every evening as they followed him out of the house toward the park.

"You'll live longer. What's wrong with you?" Victor demanded.

"Big deal," Felipe and José whined. Still, they followed him. Anything was better than lifting some dumb piece of lead. They walked silently along the quiet streets.

Upon reaching the Thruway overpass, still in single file, the boys climbed the narrow protective railing and began their familiar high-wire trek. A beaten, wounded sun about to take off for the day, black-and-blue shadows playing along the hills lining the smelly river backdropped and framed the three brothers into a massive action-edged canvas as they strolled twenty feet above a very busy Thruway. None of the boys looked down at the snarling traffic. The air was cool, almost sweet, and a trifle breezy. There was no hint of car fumes. Here was real country freshness, so the Cruzes inhaled deeply as if sucking pure oxygen. Ignoring the buzz of menacing traffic, his new Adidases squeaking in the twilight, Victor carried the NBA basketball high over his shiny afro and walked in sure confident strides. Felipe held his breath and pigeon-toed successfully but slowly across the abyss. On the final step he faked falling and almost did. José kept his eyes shut until he reached the other side. Then he bowed and high-fived Victor and Felipe.

In an antique pink Hudson, an older, slate-complexioned woman intensely watched the boys' elaborate dances across the lean overpass railing. When they started running toward the town park, the Hudson slowly picked up speed and creaked to the park entrance.

Profits from occasional street fairs had gifted outdoor furnishings to the park, thus solidifying its fragile, almost accidental, existence. The Cruzes usually tried out every toy in the park before playing basketball. All three brothers loved the sliding pond.

The old woman left her car and, with the aid of a cane, limped across the softball infield; apparently she could not take her eyes off them.

Victor whispered darkly, "The old lady's been tailing us."

"She can't be a narc."

"She can be anything. She is old enough to be anything."

"If this was South Bronx, man, her pocketbook'd been snatched and her car stripped already."

"Ok, José, ok, José, climb into her lap, too. You love crazy mamas."

The old lady was making pretty good speed. They heard the snapping of bones as she got closer; each second they thought the woman would break into many pieces. She was clearly bugged out, talking to herself and laughing.

Victor sighed uncomfortably, "Oh boy, we really get 'em."

Her washed-out blue eyes kept closing and opening at fantastic speed.

"Boys, I am Edna Malloy. I saw your act once before and caught it again today."

"We ain't got an act, lady. You made a mistake."

"What I mean, young man, is I understand that life is very easy to leave, but if you're talented, you may survive indefinitely."

"Huh?"

"Each time you walk the overpass you tempt fates and are tempted to jump, but I think you're definitely survivors. I have been one for so many years, but now I'm going to die."

"Let's get out of here," Felipe said loudly.

She turned to Victor. "Are you the oldest brother?"

Edna Malloy was very small, but her back was not bent like other old people. She stood erect and spoke like a college teacher. The boys were becoming impressed. And Victor did not fear anyone smaller than him.

"My eyes often play tricks with me, but you aren't black, are you? Your hair misled for a minute, but your coloring isn't black."

"We're Puerto Ricans."

"Good! Colored have stolen me blind in my eighty-three years."

"Us too."

"They never change. See, over there is my house, closest to the river. My home is higher than any of the old beech trees."

"Sure, oh, yeah, we see it fine."

"It was the grandest residence in town. Before I die I want it restored. I want to have a ball there."

The boys snickered.

"There used to be marvelous dances, social gatherings, and recitals in my home. My husband Edgar so loved to entertain. He was a brutal man during a working day, but in the evening he became lyrical. I feel like I've been sleeping for thirty years. When I first saw you cross the Thruway so originally, it roused me as if a young prince had awakened me. I've waited this last week for you to return."

Victor had politely stood during her monologue. His brothers lay on the grass arm-wrestling, their span of attention approximately zero. The park lights would be blinking off soon, and they were going to end up alone in the park with a fruitcup.

"You see, I want one grand party. I need your help, and I will pay competitively for your labor. Do you work?"

"We got jobs," Victor snapped defensively.

"My home is a shambles. I fear it resembles me. But it can be repaired."

"You mean paint and plaster jobs?"

"Yes. Do you do carpentry?"

Felipe answered truthfully, "We can do anything pretty good."

"I'll pay you well for a month."

"We can't just work on weekends and nights?"

"I thought you understood. I have very little time. Your wages will be two hundred dollars a week for each of you for one month."

"Sure," José grinned like a cute monkey. "Sure, we'll do it."

"I'll drive you boys home and pick you up at six tomorrow morning."

She walked in slow motion. The Cruzes graciously padded along at her pace, eager to get out of the park. What if nosy neighbors were watching right now? What if the town cop car cruised by?

"What do you call that hairstyle?"

"Afros, but we're not colored."

From cots José and Felipe bellowed to Victor who was lodged in the master bedroom. "Hey Victor, she's nuts, right?"

"Right."

"She ain't coming by at six, right?"

"I set the alarm just in case."

"Why, man?"

"Six hundred a week, man, that's why. She's bugged, but I bet she's rich."

"Aah, she's nuts."

José said, "Maybe she's a ghost like Poppa, only this time we can all see her, not just Victor."

"She's no ghost, jerk. She drives a Hudson, don't she? She may be here at six. Old people don't sleep much."

"Neither do ghosts."

"She's no ghost, José. She's the real thing."

The first two mornings Edna Malloy was on time and had to enter the sloppy apartment and wake the Cruzes, who quickly discovered she was fair but exacting. She fed them breakfast and supper ("Lunch equally dulls those who work and those who don't work"). Their beverages were freshly squeezed orange juice in the morning, ginger ale at midday, beer with supper— and, before they left at about ten in the evening, they finished off a hearty foreign wine. The Cruzes also learned that a Malloy week included working Saturdays and Sundays. The house was of good sturdy stuff and once attended even slightly, seemed to spruce up by itself. Within a week the outside trim was completed, the roof repaired, and several rooms downstairs replastered. So Edna Malloy was more than satisfied and began cooking in earnest, serving leg of lamb, roast beef, and steak. They dined at the massive oval dining table with the good silver and china. The Cruzes washed, dried, and put away all the heirloom stuff very carefully. The brothers had never been inside such an ornate home, even as delivery boys, so they were awed daily.

"It's like a damn museum. Hey, you know what, Victor?" José was jumping up and down on his cot. "Remember when you said she was the real thing?"

"So?"

"Remember the Coke commercial where an old lady is doing over her house and the whole neighborhood fixes it up while she lays Coke on 'em."

"Yeah, yeah, so?"

"I'm wondering if you ever told Poppa about her."

"I haven't seen him lately."

"Do you think he really died this time?" José asked.

"You don't make sense! You are crazy, crazier than Momma," Victor declared.

Felipe shouted out, "There's nothing in that house worth stealing too. You notice that?"

"Have you been taking anyway?" Victor growled.

Felipe wisely snorted, "Fences have no use for antiques. Only rich people buy and sell that crap."

"Nothing that is not an antique like good silver is swiped either. Understood?"

"Take it easy, big brother. I'm no junkie. I don't steal from people I like."

Overtired, each boy desperately tried to be ready for another hardworking day of restoring. Mrs. Malloy talked like no one they had ever met, and they could listen to her stories forever. And she was interested in everything, and when she laughed she only looked about sixty. They anticipated every supper because there was so much to pack away and because it was delicious and she would join them; she ate sparingly, but delighted in sitting and talking. It was fun to see her disdain a goblet and drink beer from a can. Two weeks had passed and the house was reborn, but Edna Malloy's own appearance had worsened, seemingly in proportion to the reviving of her home. She had definitely shrunk, there was no longer any color in her eyes, and her complexion was almost black, the one color she feared most. Still, she took pains in her appearance, bathed herself in perfume, always combed her hair and looked nice and neat in faded peasant dresses.

Invitations and envelopes lay on the wicker table on the porch. Felipe's turn to put away the dishes, Victor and José were smoking mild little Dutch cigars Edna had just offered.

"Can you help me address the invitations?"

"Sure."

She handed them the phone book. "Just copy down each name until you run out of envelopes. I have more upstairs."

"You mean right out of the phone book?"

"Everyone I know is dead, in a nursing home, or has moved away. I'm inviting the town," she explained softly.

"You should put an ad in the paper; it'd be much cheaper."

"But so informal, Victor. No. It's to be done this way."

"Don't you have any relatives?"

"I haven't heard from anyone in twenty years."

Felipe sauntered in. "Hey, who're you calling?"

Edna Malloy didn't pick them up the following day, so the Cruzes walked the two miles to her place; they were nervous and had not wanted to call. And they were right. For there were several police cars in her driveway. Later in the day they bought a local paper and read that Mrs. Edna Malloy, age eighty-three, had died peacefully in her sleep. She left one survivor, Andrew Malloy, residing in Lincoln, Nebraska. They decided not to go to the funeral home or to the funeral. Two days later they visited the cemetery, sat around her grave, grinned foolishly, and left flowers and a bottle of wine.

According to the terms of her will, the Cruz brothers received the Hudson plus two paid-off years of car insurance. The nephew from Nebraska immediately sold the property. Three weeks later the Cruzes were hired to help demolish the house and erect another condominium. They drove the Hudson to work every day and apparently saw nothing strange or ironic about what they had just rebuilt. But they never drove the Hudson to the park. They always set out on foot as before and, reaching the overpass, highwired effortlessly. They now looked down and mocked the dumb traffic—to walk that highwire was as simple as hissing out one's next breath. They would never fall from that narrow railing's grace.

Felipe

THE ghost of Raymondo Cruz began to finally understand that everything is elusive and fleeting. Body and mind breakdowns apparently were to be his universal lot. Raymondo's eyes blurred and his shaky legs could barely function, let alone fly. He was absent from the apartment for weeks at a time, not because he was drunk or had forsaken them, but simply because he had forgotten where they lived.

Poppa perfunctorily summed up debits and credits. Victor was destined to be just another face in a faceless crowd. José had unfortunately misused his capacity for leadership. The boy was not a revolutionary; his oratory and hallucinations only excited girls who thought him a poet. But Felipe was always in disfavor.

Raymondo recalled now he and Maria both had battered that cranky colicky child. Twice Maria had tried to throw Felipe out the window; twice the father snatched the screaming infant from the mad woman; and more than twice Poppa was sorry he had intervened. Today the ghost despaired, for Felipe had not made any significant steps toward a peaceful survival. Despite his size and great strength, Felipe remained merely a nasty, dangerous bully.

Felipe trusted no one but his brothers, yet he was surly and unemotional to Victor and José, and very quick to mock their flaws and errors. They in turn only tolerated Felipe because he was their brother. Raymondo Cruz had stared piercingly into the soul of that doltish, slow-thinking brute and saw that Felipe was consumed by a love for his brothers that would never be articulated or demonstrated. Felipe was also the one fool who could one day pack a gun and try the desperate holdup like his Poppa. He too would be slammed into a useless pile of dead flesh, too dumb to even become a ghost. Now when Poppa did remember the correct address, he only talked of Felipe's future. Often he became rambling and incoherent. Victor always tried to be polite, but sometimes became very impatient at the silly conversation.

Poppa confessed, "Felipe is always in my thoughts and dreams."

Victor teased, "Wait till I tell Felipe he's your favorite."

"Yes, my son, do tell him. He may not believe it since it's not true, yet you have no reason to taunt him, so it may make an impression."

"Only a tractor's wheels could dent him."

"I respect all man's jobs, but he is always a brutal bouncer at bars and dance halls. To inflict pain, to only reveal one's muscles and strength, is like a dirty striptease."

"Not the same, Poppa."

"The same for me."

"Why do you suddenly care for him?" Victor was

only half teasing. The old man never showed up much anymore, and when he did, he talked dopey.

"I worry. What if you get evicted from here?"

"Why should we? Calm yourself."

"You're Puerto Rican. Reason enough to worry."

"We pay our rent."

"Suppose they raise it?"

"Worry then."

"It is an eternal miracle you three lived in the same orphanage and now in the same apartment, safe from New York City. I feel some way responsible for your good fortune."

Victor smirked, "We thank you, Poppa, for what you've done. Rest easy. You've done enough."

The ghost warned, "But I will not always be around," and he added, "for I am very sick."

"Hah, *you!*"

"Believe it. Don't I appear dimmer?"

"The lighting stinks. We got no bulbs."

"Well I am much, much dimmer. My voice is but a sigh. Soon I will need a stick to guide me. My eyes are only rotting holes. When you leave here, you must look out for Felipe. He is the weakest of the mutts and will fall apart if left alone."

"The whole neighborhood is afraid of him."

"You know nothing of the world or the neighborhood," the old man gently chided.

"Enough to know that when Felipe walks into a store everyone runs."

"What good to your heart if you only strike fear into others?"

"I wouldn't mind."

"He is frightened of his power because to him it is no power."

"Felipe is scared of being a bully?"

"Yes."

"Poppa, he has nothing else but strength—what are you going to do?"

Raymondo Cruz was struck down. He lost the sight of his left eye, he limped, and his body shook convulsively every other second. He stumbled along suburban streets moaning in pain and crying tears of frustration. Felipe's strength was a cancer and must somehow be exorcised. The father tripped into an alley and tried to sleep the rest of the day away.

Walking back home from a disco late at night, Felipe saw a sight that both attracted him and made him back off. Peeing against a garbage can was a three-legged dog. Felipe laughed and turned away. The dog followed him as best it could. Felipe tried to ignore what was following him. When he got outside his apartment, he warned the dog to get lost. The dog balanced itself precariously, just listening. It was the ugliest thing Felipe had ever seen. No one else was on the block, so Felipe unzipped and hosed down the creature with a stream of hot urine. The mutt fell down whining, and Felipe restrained himself from kicking it.

Engulfed in delirium, the ghost of Raymondo Cruz awoke to some tottering awkward beast peeing on his cuffless zip pants. He also spied Felipe, and followed the two strange beasts. Raymondo was unsure whether this was all a dream, but what does it matter—the signs, the symbols matter. He pressed on. It didn't take Raymondo long to plan, decide, and act.

First he attempted an even greater miracle the next morning and tried to speak to Felipe, who was watching a TV cartoon. The boy gave no sign of hearing what the father tried to explain. Then the ghost of Raymondo Cruz floated to the TV set and turned it off. When Felipe approached the set, the father, crossing himself several times, leaped at his son and bit deeply into Felipe's right arm. Felipe fainted with the second bite. However, Poppa attacked the arm twice more, then calmly waited around until José and Victor returned. They phoned the cops, who called the ambulance, and everybody sped off.

Felipe's shrunken arm resembled a fantastic rainbow; first it was red, then yellow, green, blue, and then it stayed black for two days. When Felipe regained consciousness, the arm was American white, not Rican tan, and it was withered and half the size of the left arm. There were no marks at all, so the doctor concealed his ignorance by loudly proclaiming a short circuit must have done it—but didn't make clear what that meant. A day later he gently explained to Felipe that the arm was not completely useless. Felipe would be able to use a knife and fork and write very slowly and perform other easy tasks. Felipe, remembering the pain, was content not to be in the morgue.

José and Victor never left their brother's side. Victor lost his job for staying two consecutive days, but José was deep in welfare conniving and laying a young secretary who sent him double checks, so things were ok. They did not mention Felipe's arm at the hospital, nor did they ever mention it at home. Strangers began to smile in pity. Felipe grinned back. Who could remember when Felipe's eyes were not dusty or dark? Now they had lightened considerably, and the skin texture around his eyes and mouth softened.

The ghost of Raymondo Cruz left his gift at the door. Felipe leaned down to help the three-legged dog to an erratic posture. Felipe patted the dog with his withered hand and felt a flickering of life in the palm. He patted the dog—again the flash of liveliness. The dog licked Felipe's palm and now his fingers reached out like the petals of a flower, reaching for the sun. Felipe immediately saw the dog was magic and brought it into the apartment. Nobody argued.

A week later, Felipe named the dog Mucho. The ghost of Raymondo Cruz, deep in the confines of the grimy hallway, had observed everything and decided not to caution Felipe, who couldn't hear him anyway. He wrote in invisible graffiti on the already crowded walls: *and my son if you would touch the animal's stump, it too would experience some sensation and await the return of a fourth leg that will never arrive. Neither will your arm noticeably improve, but as long as you touch one another you have only lost power, but found love. At least that is the way I think.*

For a week Raymondo Cruz suffered ferocious headaches, but when the massive migraines vanished, complete vision showed up at the darkened left eye. Suddenly the ghost's mind was clear and pure, and finally, with astonishment and great pride, the old man noticed his sleepy penis saluting the pretty girls once more.

Mr. Collision

While he lived, Raymondo Cruz was awed by and drawn to men who were worthy public speakers, con men who could package anger and humor to lasso a crowd of drifters and make them into an effective team, a force to be reckoned with. Words were magic when strung together. Raymondo was a terrific listener and hearing outstanding speakers and planners, like the Cortez family, was a beautiful experience. It was like golden clothes hanging on a line, sparkling in a sweet breeze: the sight and sounds of flapping clean clothes was sensational. Nothing was impossible when you were led by words. Raymondo was easily incited and inflamed more than once in the Bronx. Pedro Cortez had talked Raymondo and others into signing up for dish-washing jobs in the Catskills, and though Raymondo and the others knew the pay was poor and the living conditions even worse, the Cortezian words were gentle swords, able to protect you. So Raymondo trucked every year to the Catskills. After two or three weeks, he stumbled back to the Bronx, sheepish and penniless. But now Raymondo was very excited again by the potential arrival of another Cortez. What a family! Besides the poor, the Cortezes had hoodwinked mayors and governors!

Jorge Cortez was in the country. Apocryphal Cortez stories roamed all over the Bronx and many sections of Manhattan and Brooklyn. Relatives had been successful con men in so many neighborhoods, it seemed inevitable a Cortez would come to the country.

Jorge Cortez would zoom away from his beloved Bronx social club, speed over the bridge, and up the pretty parkway to seek strong Spanish warriors. All a recruiter had to do was loiter around the gates of the Sacred Home for Fallen Angels and the orphans would empty the institution to apply. Also, Jorge would hear about those who had graduated or been canned from Sacred Home and now lived nearby, scraping by. But Jorge could change all that scuffling. His pencil would tear at the lined notebook slashing out so many damn names.

And the Cruz boys knew Jorge Cortez would soon be dropping by. So Felipe, with his one mighty arm, quickly vacuumed the apartment and relegated his dusting to a slightly withered left arm. José sent out for beer as Victor placed the fruit—two lemons, a black-and-blue orange, four bananas, and a dozen bitterly sour cherries—into a large salad bowl. Three-legged Mucho, nervous at the energetic activity, peed twice on the bathroom mat.

Rumors filtered in for two days. The nuns had chased Jorge with big brooms and shook gnarled fists and crucifixes at his descending Buick convertible. But Jorge was all smiles, blessing them, blowing kisses, backing down the sloping hill, for he got what he came for. Names, names, names: available young Puerto Ricans to join his sorties against the establishment. The Cruz brothers could hardly wait for Jorge to arrive at their place: he represented the closest they would ever get to big-time crime. All sorts of rumors haloed Jorge Cortez. A long-time claim was that the Cortez family had a Jewish lawyer in the till who would always bail you out, even during the Sabbath or any holy Jewish day or night.

The brothers were polite and shy when Jorge meekly knocked at the door. They offered cold beer and fruit and then passed around a fat-assed joint. Jorge accepted every gift graciously, but he wet-lipped the joint so badly it came apart and its precious contents floated onto the floor. The boys shrugged and smiled dumbly.

Physically, Jorge Cortez was a severe disappointment. He was very tall and very skinny; no shoulders, but equipped with an unusually thick, knotted neck which resembled a snake swollen with fresh pig. Jorge had the biggest Adam's apple in the world, and José kept staring at it. Jorge shrugged a great deal, as if he understood he was quite a sight. Felipe almost snickered, and Victor tried to sweep up the grass and package the remnants. The ghost of Raymondo Cruz, mourning gross in-breeding, scanned Jorge to find some clue that he was indeed a Cortez, but came up empty. Raymondo felt like a plant circling about, looking for a place to land. Below were only mountains and a stormy ocean, and he was going to run out of gas very soon.

"You guys a real family, heh?"

"Yeh."

"All over you see families plotting against each other, ya know. It's sick."

José said, "We're all we got."

"You guys are solid."

Victor beamed, "You want another beer?"

"Nah. Look, you know what I'm doing here?"

They nodded.

"Looking around. My scouting report says there are plenty of tough, smart guys up here. I didn't find any till I got here."

Victor said, "We don't do mugging, you know."

"Hey, I only mug cars. You know the word for my success, my secret word? I'll tell you in a minute."

Felipe burped and left the room to get another beer. Munching on a lemon, Jorge waited for him to return and then gently touched Felipe's limp right hand.

"There's room for everybody when we mug cars. A guy like you standing around, Felipe, makes a busybody less nervous."

Felipe looked away and patted Mucho, who was still shivering at the sight of Jorge.

"Keep talking," Victor encouraged. "What do you do exactly?"

"You know the Cortez family name is famous in the Bronx. As famous as Columbus."

"We don't know him either. What's the secret word anyway?"

"Yeah."

"The magic word," Jorge said quickly now, "is collision."

"Collision?"

The ghost mourned and mourned.

"Collision shops are around more than McDonalds. I supply them with parts, all kinds of fresh living car parts. After they tow a wreck, they call me and I fill the order and everybody makes money, money."

"How come they call you? I worked for a collision guy. We never called you," Victor grumbled.

"I am," he said modestly, "Mr. Collision. But not in this county."

"How many shops got your number?"

"More than you can count."

"No shit."

"I'll teach you how to stake out a street and how to farm a car. *Farm* is the modern word we use now. And then you'll know everything and be my gang up here. But first, how about a present from me to you?"

José said half nervously, "Hey, I don't want a transmission in the living room."

"This is better than a four-speed transmission," Jorge pulled out a few certificates.

"They're phony. You won't have to pay insurance, just write in your car's name."

Victor sighed, "Thanks."

"My garage for stripping cars is right over the bridge. It runs along the turnpike and superhighway, so how can I miss with my prices? More wrecks around than rapes. You can look it up."

None of the brothers offered their beds to Jorge who accepted the floor happily.

"In a few days we begin."

Jorge talked a blue streak the following day, admitting that some of his uncles had recently deceived migrant blueberry workers in New Jersey and apple pickers further upstate New York. Some of the Cortez legend was a hindrance that Jorge was trying to level down.

"In a way I'm glad I speak poorly. My uncles are mostly con men and there are ill feelings against us, especially in Brooklyn." Jorge had a fake credit card and granted it to the Cruzes while he used their facilities.

As days passed, Jorge seemed to be going nowhere but to sleep. When he did awake, Jorge asked Felipe to

MR. COLLISION

write out a shopping list, and then Jorge found a gourmet shop that would accept his credit card and he brought back nothing that was on Felipe's list. The Cruzes swiftly found themselves dwarfed by mounds of imported cheese, tins of caviar and fat sardines, and weird-looking sausages. They found most of the items tasteless and inedible.

Jorge snored and ranted in his sleep. He used the bathroom excessively. He was, however, a hard man to dislike, but you could get annoyed. Since his arm had withered, Felipe's cruel disposition had considerably sweetened. Still, even he was getting pissed at the gawky intruder. José began to mimic their guest and only Victor's poise kept everything in reasonable check and balance. Meanwhile, the ghost of Raymondo Cruz prayed and prayed that his sons would not get messed up by this loser. If he'd been Jewish, Raymondo would've sat on a frail wooden crate and torn his clothes, wailing at the dismal future.

The boys were getting very hungry. They could not swallow the vile-looking caviar, and they gingerly handled the imported cheeses which were greasy like soft butter. There was no money in the house; the last welfare check had been cashed weeks ago.

"Have nothing to do with this man. He's not a true Cortez, and he speaks like a greaser immigrant," Poppa told Victor.

"Yeah, yeah, he's a Cortez lemon, but his ideas about cars are interesting."

"Beware, my son. Americans care more about their cars than family. They will kill you for sitting on the hood. I have seen such sights."

"Poppa, everyone has insurance now. If we steal a car, they'll get a newer model. Nobody gets hurt."

MR. COLLISION

"Stay away from him. He's a leper."
"He's just tired."
"Or frightened."
"He's no liar, and I think cars are his trade. He's got Cortez blood. It'll work out."
"Never! Such noble blood has been watered down. Look at his shape!"
"Poppa! I don't dump on a Puerto Rican unless I have to."

Jorge was pouring honey and English currants into an Irish scone while Felipe dreamed of grape jelly and gummy Wonder Bread, when Victor walked into the kitchen and said, "Ok Jorge, we want action, we need it. Let's go today."
"Not today," Jorge corrected. "Tonight at midnight from twelve to five in the morning. That's when citizens sleep. I was waiting for you to be impatient, so we begin tonight." His voice had become deeper, no longer shrill. "My garage craftsmen wait for our success up here. I like to deal with skilled labor, you know. Once I tried counterfeiting. . . ."
"Yeah, what happened?"
"One mistake: our etcher was color-blind. Who knew until it was too late—the finest equipment and a true craftsman, but who can use purple ten-dollar bills?"
"Only a faggot."
"Before I go back to sleep," Jorge said, "Tell me where is the richest and newest development."
They told him.
That night at ten after twelve, they drove slowly down to Rivercrest Hills. Jorge chose a street only five

MR. COLLISION

blocks away from a highway. They spied a pretty black Oldsmobile in a driveway.

Jorge said, "That's the car. Here's our farm; we park here and watch." Nothing much to see, two men walked their dogs, and then all the house lights were snapped off. Hours later they drove back home.

The following evening the same lack of action and Jorge explained, "Victor and José, wait in my car further up the block. Me and Felipe get out and approach the Olds. I shove in the small window on the driver's side . . ."

"Cool."

"Then I reach in and pull down the big window and I climb in. That way no alarm goes off since a door is never opened. Then I pull down the other big window and in comes Felipe."

"I can dig it."

"Next, I have my own ignition set plus key. We pull out the wires of the old ignition and connect the wires to my toy and I turn my key."

"And fuck, we're off."

"Not yet. Victor flashes his brake lights two times if it's ok. Then we start going slowly. We keep the Olds' lights off until we get on the highway."

Victor smiled, for here was a smooth Cortez line. He hoped Poppa was around listening to this. Everything was going to be fine.

"Where do we go?"

"Next stop, my garage, where you boys get one hundred dollars."

"From you?"

"From my safe at the garage."

"When do we go, man?"

"Tomorrow."

"This is cool."
"Like a damn movie. No fuck up, right?"
"How can there be?"

The following evening, the residents again went to bed early. Only one development guy walked his dog while they waited. There was a sound of trucks hurtling by on the nearby highway. The homes at Rivercrest were very big and modern and their A-shaped roofs pricked the starry sky. Jorge Cortez clapped his hands loudly.

Jorge and Felipe got in the Olds quick as hell. Victor signaled it was ok. Jorge started up the car and slowly began to follow Victor, who unaccountably backed up the Buick and crashed into the Olds. There was a tearing, hooking sound, and the two cars were attached and rolled from side to side. Dogs were barking, lights were going on, but nobody was stepping outside, yet.

There were many cries of *Shit, Shit,* from both autos. The cars, now coupled firmly, spun together onto a lawn. More lights and people were looking out, but nobody stepped outside.

Jorge said, "Ok, run like hell, run like hell."

The four cops came, two from either end of the block. José, the last to leave, did the only smart thing left for him to do. Up the beech tree he scampered like a rabid squirrel. He didn't stop until he was on top of the fucking thing and looked down and listened.

" . . . damn kids."
"Vandals . . ."
"Even here."

A lady screamed, "Our lawn, we just seeded it. Look at our fucking lawn."

José giggled as the woman started to really curse. One of the four cops had his gun out and was holding it

MR. COLLISION

in the air like it was a balloon, then the cop stroked the gun like it was part of his body. Shit, what a jerk! José almost obeyed an impulse to spit down at the guy. Soon everyone got tired and bored and it was silent again. José scampered down the beech tree and began jogging toward the highway.

At breakfast Jorge was very calm and forgiving, and he patted Victor again and again.

"Forget it. Errors are part of the game."

"I'm sorry about your car."

José was setting the table, and Felipe was bringing imported jelly, Irish soda bread, and tea biscuits to the table.

"Boy, did we mess up."

"Nah, I've been in worse situations. Frankly, it happens to me a lot. Once," Jorge said, "we staked out a car and when we were driving outta the neighborhood, I see one of the citizens getting mugged, so I stopped the car and we beat up the two blacks who are mugging. The cops come and we are congratulated and everybody forgets that we jumped out of a car that wasn't ours. So we backed away and took off in the car we came in and left the hit car. Too bad, but you know I staked out the place a week and had a feeling for the citizens who lived there. Those black muggers kept looking at us like we were crazy Spics."

"Which you were," Victor said. "That's a great story, Jorge."

"Thanks. Don't you guys want soda bread?"

Felipe said glumly, and nobody laughed, "Soda is to drink."

Jorge, minus his car, took the bus back to the Bronx, but never got there in one piece. His ride was aborted by a blind-side tackle by a rival bus company. Jorge was

MR. COLLISION

hauled away with two broken legs and a roaring headache, which netted him a hefty out-of-court settlement. So Jorge Cortez recuperated in Puerto Rico and every few weeks mailed a pretty postcard to the boys. Once he sent José a purple ten-dollar bill which José taped up in the messy kitchen.

Felipe cradled the dog in his arms crooning softly.

Victor announced, "We need A & P crap. We work awhile. I am going to a job in maintenance at the high school. They need that prison spic-and-span before school starts up. You hire on as short-order cook at the diner and José will be your dishwasher."

"How long we gotta work, Victor?"

"We work awhile. I guarantee you we will dump out all this rich food and fill the place with supermarket crap."

"Ok."

"There's a damn inflation, so we work awhile."

"Ok."

They grinned at one another and started slapping each other five. Nobody spoke for a few minutes.

Finally Victor said, "I'll walk the dog for you, Felipe."

"Ok, thanks. I'll do the dishes. You dry 'em, José."

Victor reached for the leash and the dog was all over him.

"Don't rush him, Victor. Mucho'll do his business, but he is nervous, so don't bark at him," Felipe cautioned.

"I don't dump on crippled mutts," Victor said softly.

Outside, the air was fresh with only an occasional smell of fumes and dog shit. Mucho was sniffing near, and Victor patiently waited for the dog to move around.

107

MR. COLLISION

The light emanating from the lamppost seemed to be blinking in some sort of pattern that Victor didn't care to decipher. He looked down at the base of the post and saw Mucho taking his crap. The turds were shaped like letters, but he didn't read them, either. The light returned now into a pure crime-deterrent glare. Victor and Mucho started back home, the dog struggling vainly to keep up with Victor's fast pace. When they got back, Victor gallantly opened the front door and let Mucho in. The dog slunk in expecting the worst, but Victor only took off the leash and permitted the dog to proceed at its own deliberate pace into their home.

The Apartment

In the beginning the apartment was packed high with new cassettes, a host of 45's, a sensational stereo (bought from a desperate junkie), and a good TV in a broken chassis. There were plenty of throw pillows, busted couches, love seats, and one rocking chair. All the possessions were obtained from rummage sales or simply ripped off in imaginative ways.

In the beginning everything took root in the living room and it sometimes appeared that a benevolent sun lit up the place twenty-four hours a day. The apartment was a magical merry funhouse tunnel, and the Cruz boys were the ticket sellers, guides, and wide-eyed tourists. The apartment was a promised land immigrants only see in the mist of great dreams.

But after a splendid beginning comes the disruptive middle. For the moment, all the brothers' earned wages and money were no longer tossed into a common pot. Felipe, Victor, and José no longer ate meals together. They hid food in their sloppy rooms. Everyone had a TV. Raymondo Cruz, terribly wise in the breakup of the family, spotted many other flaws and could not keep still any longer.

"Oh, the living room is bare, my son. There is a TV now in each bedroom."

"Where they belong, Poppa."

"I preferred it the other way."

"But it don't make no sense, three TVs banging away at the same time in the same room, sometimes all tuned to the same station. It was more like Momma's crazy place. With the stereo and radio going full blast, I kept thinking we're back in the South Bronx."

The ghost winced.

"We need privacy. We're getting older; only you stay the same."

The ghost made no reply.

"Also, Poppa, though we are all Cruzes, we laugh at different jokes. We're different."

"All that noise is life," the old man weakly countered.

"We're not city punks. We like it pretty quiet sometimes."

"Noise can mean happiness, my son."

"And silence can mean you're happy and content, too. We're different, Poppa," the boy said softly, feeling sorry for the nervous old man.

Like any disappointed parent, Raymondo stubbornly repeated himself.

"You spend so little time together with your brothers."

Victor could no longer be polite.

"I gotta go now. We'll talk again."

The ghost of Raymondo Cruz fondly remembered Bronx tenements and forlorn crowds, glass-littered streets, and the angry shouts ricocheting day and night; the jettisoning hydrants, false alarms, the cold

THE APARTMENT

beers, the warm sweet wine. But all was a private, self-contained, selfish flashback. Victor, José, and Felipe quested for a sedate middle-class status while he, a bullet-ridden ghost, a stubborn jackass, sometimes longed for the frenzied lifestyle. Though proud of their choice, the father felt definitely estranged. But of even greater significance and importance, the ghost realized the apartment itself was in danger of becoming vacant.

In October, a Christmas card from the administration of Sacred Home of Fallen Angels arrived, not only wishing all its ex-orphans the merriest of holiday seasons, but inviting one and all back for a day of repast and prayer. Previously it was the sullen Home policy to deal perfunctorily and pitilessly with its wards, and once the children graduated or reached the age of eighteen, to deal with them not at all. Children who tried the patience of the quick-to-get-angry-and-disgusted nuns were drop-kicked out, swiftly (both José and Felipe went that route), while those who stubbornly survived were, upon graduation, usually herded together and flung on a chartered bus to New York. Victor had been shrewd enough to ignore that sinister invitation. Sacred Home for Fallen Angels never aided those who tried to make it nearby. Anyone seen on the grounds of the Home was considered trespassing, and the police were summoned. *Making it,* according to the social worker philosophy, was living in the Bronx and dying a lot or a little each day. Others rebelled less successfully than the Cruzes. Last winter some ex-orphans camped out in the forest behind the Home. The poor lost souls foraged and stole from the Home canteen and garbage to eke out a pathetic existence. But eventually a sharp-eyed nun spied them, and the police locked up the marauding band for a week and warned them to stay out of the county. Victor and his brothers still considered Sacred Home their home. It was the only place, except for the apartment, where they had been warm and fed three times a day. It had few ingredients of a real home, yet the boys hung on foolishly and stubbornly to the false trappings. And now came the invitation to come back. Not to sneak back, but come through the front door. None of the brothers could really believe the invitation was not some sort of prank. Neither could they wait to attend.

The brothers planned what to wear, debated whether to bring gifts, and guessed what the Home wanted from them anyway. The ghost of Raymondo Cruz was a correct man, and he disliked even *true* blasphemous statements about the Church and its servants. But he said nothing to Victor because the note had drawn the brothers together again. Whether they noticed it or not, they now usually went into Victor's room and watched his TV after supper as they recounted savage childhood Sacred Home anecdotes. The boys sometimes touched each other as they fought to tell their tales. The ghost was pleased. Though still not noisy, the apartment again smelled of cooking and wine and joints, and Poppa was content and noticed everything.

"How we getting to the Home—taxi?"

"Taxi on the way back. We'll take a bus now."

José and Felipe groaned.

"C'mon, Victor, why take that shit bus? We still gotta walk plenty when we get off."

"That's tough, José."

Felipe butted in, "Yeah, and that county bus comes once a year."

"Right! So let's get started."

THE APARTMENT

José grumbled, "Victor'd be cheap even if he had big bucks."

Poppa chose not to stay in the apartment or go with his sons. He loved the sounds of bowling balls crushing tenpins, so he drifted toward a nearby bowling alley.

Victor's only suit was a discounted polyester two-piece from Marshall's. By the time Victor reached the bus stop, the suit looked as if it'd been slept in. José's Calvin Klein cargo pants featured many deep pockets, all empty. An emerald green extra-large polo hung like a curtain, almost touching José's sandals, but he didn't mind since Ralph Lauren's logo was affixed to that garment. Felipe, looking even chubbier than he was, wore a canary yellow leisure suit, a memento of an aborted criminal career.

The bus was late. A time schedule for the County Bus Line did not exist, but if one waited long enough, a ratty, noisy bus tottered by. For a flat fee of sixty cents CBL drivers, never in uniform, usually sporting scruffy beards and always smoking cigarettes, took passengers anywhere along a fifteen-mile stretch of Route 79. Since there were no designated bus stops, the CBL paused anywhere, though the usual destination was the Mall and its mutt litter of shops. However, like bad dreams, grimy stores and fast food joints herded together the entire length of 79. The highway ended at the edge of a state-owned forest that no passenger ever entered.

Finally, a CBL vehicle chugged into view. An amiable driver welcomed the brothers. They dashed to the back.

José laughed, "I just hope we get there by tomorrow."

Twenty minutes later, they disembarked and began trudging past bankrupt garages and custard stands,

THE APARTMENT

then circled a small, musty development with narrow driveways cluttered with cars and bikes. Nobody talked. Though the hike was not demanding, it seemed all the Cruzes had decided to save their energy. It was dusk. Several stars crept out; the moon, more like a fragile silhouette, slid into place. José whistled. Felipe sang to himself. Victor was all business, the lead scout concerned about stray watchdogs or a busybody cop car.

Reaching a familiar hill, they sighed in unison, climbed it quickly, and then ran down the other side, anticipating the landscape. But everything had changed. José wished he had binoculars to make sure this was the right Sacred Home.

"Is that all there was?" Felipe muttered in a puzzled, hurt tone.

Victor pointed out that several buildings must've been demolished and the pieces tossed away. The old crumbling Recreation Hall was definitely gone. A few of the cottages remained; others had vanished.

Felipe and José started punching each other playfully. As they neared the Home, they became less agitated, happily recognizing several statues, the church, and the parking lots.

José shouted, "There's a lot more cars now. That's where the fuckin' lawn went! They paved everything down to make more parking spaces."

Felipe agreed. "Remember when Sister Noreen had fits if anybody, staff or visitor, ever parked in the wrong space?"

José giggled. "Yeah, she sounded the fire alarm! What a great cop Sister Noreen woulda made. She'd be writing tickets twenty-four hours a day."

Victor saw that their cottage was padlocked and the grass around it hadn't been mowed for a couple of seasons. He doubted his counselor, Billy Murphy, was still around.

What, he wondered, if it's all a trap just to round us up? Like the Nazis did years ago. But that was crazy. The new security guards looked like marshmallow salesmen. And there were neat signs all over the grounds inviting the guests to meet in the new Cultural Center. There're no trucks or buses around to pack us into. I guess it's ok, Victor thought, and finally relaxed. After all, we used to live here.

The boys felt relieved when they spotted Ramos and Hernandez, arch-enemies long ago.

"Was there a jail break? What are you guys doing here?" Hernandez joked nastily. They warily gave each other high fives, but their voices never became boisterous. Sacred Home still retained genuine power over the orphans.

Ramos warned, "It don't matter if nuns don't dress like nuns anymore, they're still around and still the same."

José said, "We lasted, too."

Ramos whispered something to Hernandez, and they laughed at the Cruz brothers. Felipe was getting annoyed but said nothing. Victor saw the two guys hadn't gained any weight or improved their personalities.

"It smelled better years ago," Victor declared.

"Bullshit, it never smelled right," Ramos argued and glared at Victor.

"It could be like a camp here," José sighed.

"Yeah, but it wasn't, pretty boy," Hernandez said, winking at José.

Felipe snarled, "Shut up, dickheads."

Ramos gave him the finger. "You guys were always nuts."

THE APARTMENT

Cradling his useless arm, Felipe advised strongly, "Keep walking, assholes."

In the windowless Cultural Center, under dim lighting, Sister Noreen, in a black jumper, stood on stage, arms crossed, looking for trouble. The rowdy audience quickly shut up. Sister thanked the wards for coming. José and Felipe whispered loudly. Sister Noreen noticed and flashed them a wicked look. Victor smiled, for this was like the good old days. Then Sister Noreen introduced a fat caseworker who revealed that Sacred Home was in disrepair. The speaker smiled weakly and the audience listened warily. There was much carpentry and roofing to be done and, since these young men and women had profited from the Home experience, it was only natural that many future weekends should be claimed for free services.

"You have to be here Saturday morning and out Sunday night," the social worker proclaimed and then curtly dismissed them.

The audience rose immediately and left. Happily accepting the lack of grace, the wards reassured each other.

"Sacred Home hasn't changed. It's the same, the fuckin' same. Why should it ever change?"

Sad, but delighted, all raced outside where a hundred stars criss-crossed the black sky.

The door to the apartment was ajar. Victor smiled nervously at his brothers. Felipe pushed past Victor and shoved open the door. They all grunted and they sighed. The apartment was practically bare; they'd been ripped off. All the couches, shag rugs, records, silverware, tables, plus hockables were taken.

THE APARTMENT

"Someone just furnished their apartment," José sighed, giggling a little.

"Hey," Felipe questioned. "Were we rich, Victor?"

"Yeah, yeah, we were rich. We musta been. They really took from us. I bet they were white dudes, too. We gotta get better police protection in this neighborhood, hot damn."

Victor too was smiling. Cowering in the corner was Mucho. Felipe caressed the scared animal.

"Hey, Mucho, we got robbed!"

José said, "We're going to be really busy fixing up Sacred Home and this place again! Boy!"

The father, leaning against a wall, marveled at their calmness and happily listened to their grandiose plans for restocking the apartment. Victor talked glibly of buying insurance next time, and Felipe discussed burglar locks. It was like a town meeting as they considered many ways of keeping those poorer than they were "the hell outta here." The brothers even sang a little, though all the liquor was gone and so were the glasses. With their fists, the Cruzes toasted new plans and dreams. Even the dumb dog seemed no longer tense and vainly attempted a three-legged pavan for the giddy boys.

"They took everything, almost," Victor pointed out, and the boasting and toasting continued all night. Just before dawn, as his sons slept on the living room floor, legs entwined about each other, the ghost of Raymondo Cruz danced the bossa nova with Mucho. The ghost and the crippled mutt glided effortlessly to the simple tunes of celebration.

Three Points

Victor had played soccer in high school. First he played goal, then defense. In his senior year he was shifted to wing and became an opportunistic scorer. He'd cut out newspaper clippings claiming "Cruz Is Key to Attack." Eventually he lost the articles, but he still fondly remembered the headlines about his exploits.

Once out of the Home, Victor played no more soccer. He shot baskets with his brothers, and the trio managed to fend off most challengers to the court. But now Felipe, favoring a maimed arm, avoided playing basketball, claiming he could no longer properly elbow and rebound. José disliked sweating too much and no longer accompanied Victor to the nearby park.

Now, instead of a basketball, Victor brought along a scuffed, punctured soccerball and practiced. "Good foot, good foot," he called out to himself as he aimed his kicks between the swings and small sandbox. The ball was high enough to clear the swings, but not high enough to soar over the protective wire fence circling

THREE POINTS

the edge of the park. Below was the Thruway and its kamikaze flow of rushing traffic.

With fall weather, Victor decided to try place-kicking and requisitioned José to rip off a kicking tee and football from the sporting goods center. Now he returned to the park each night after work, after supper, to practice and perfect his unique form. It was essential not to lose the damn ball. Victor disdained trying to kick in a slashing sideways soccer thrust, but if he kicked the ball head on, it would surely dart over the fence and be immediately deflated by the cars below. So the young man sat down on the grass and pondered it out. Here was a special problem that he perceived clearly. The options were diagrammed in his mind, and it was not easy to concentrate with such a sweet buttery breeze licking his face. The hum of traffic was tranquilizing and he almost napped. Instead, Victor solved the dilemma and developed a sneaky approach, dubbed his sneak hump try. It was a quick half-step right up to the football, then willing all his strength into his toes, he curled toward the pigskin and there it went, lofting way high in the sky, soaring over the swings and then descending like a felled bird in front of the protective fence. The next thirty kicks were exactly the same. "Good hump, good hump," he kept saying. Victor shook hands with himself. He knew he had something, but he wasn't quite sure what he could do with this new skill.

Few people used the park in the evening, but Champ Melvin's twin girls could usually con their father into swinging them for a while. Champ was a very skinny, bony, broken-nosed man who made a lot of money in shady real-estate dealing. He loved only his family and the Holy Grail pursuit of becoming a big shot. In politics, he remained a behind-the-scenes meddler and fixer, but could never run for an office since he absolutely lacked charisma and had no hint of sincerity. He was the kind of hack named by cronies to committees and other token posts. His beady eyes and crooked grin more than hinted that Champ could be bought and was willing to buy added power. Champ accepted the bleak truth that even in a small town like Ripley he must remain on the edge of genuine public renown. Then one cool evening, Adolph Grupp, the chief of police and former head coach of Ripley High School, strolled up to the Melvin porch.

Chief Grupp told Champ there was a semi-pro league working out of Brooklyn and New Jersey looking for franchises in the country.

"Champ, we got the makings of a contender. All our ex-high-school stars just lounge around town, you know, work for the utility company, go into construction, become cops, or they just don't do anything. We can field a representative team. I'll coach, you be the president. We'll make the frigging playoffs. I swear we will."

Champ smiled, "It sounds good."

"We can fill Ripley Stadium. The people will want to see again those seventeen-year-olds who thrilled them years ago."

Champ added, "We can get free publicity from the local radio station and paper. How much will it cost to get a franchise?"

"Not much. Champ, we only pay the players on a bonus performance scale. They'll mostly be playing for nothing, except for the stars."

Champ nodded, but didn't say anything. Grupp added the clincher.

"Champ, you hold the ball for extra points and field goals."

"I'd be the holder," Champ repeated modestly, dumbly, and happily.

"You'll be the president and pay our bills?"

"Ok."

"Then you're my damn holder into the Super Bowl."

The next evening Champ returned to the little park with his daughters.

"Daddy, there's that funny man again."

But Champ already knew *he* was there. He'd seen that Spic booting the ball in a silly, twitching movement, but the damn ball was a perfect arc every damn time, at least fifty times an evening.

Champ walked across the field to where the kid was practicing. Champ's daughters, howling in mock fear, happily followed their dad.

"Hey, kid."

"Yeah?"

"I'll hold the ball for you."

"The tee's ok."

"Let me hold it once."

"Ok." Victor eyed him suspiciously.

"I'm a professional holder."

"What team?"

"The Ripley Red Raiders."

"Don't know 'em."

"They're a new local team. I'm the holder and president. You live around here?"

"Sure."

Champ held the ball and didn't feel Victor's toes nudge the pigskin. It orbited obediently into the air, then flew the required distance, and landed carefully near the fence. It was as if a computer had kicked the damn ball.

"You do that every time?"
"Yeah."
"That's three points," Champ explained.
"Yeah, three points in this dumpy park." Champ's girls laughed.
Champ corrected gently, "And anywhere else in the country, kid. It's still three points. What's your handle?"
"Cruz, Victor Cruz."
"I'm Melvin. Champ Melvin, and I want you to try out for the Red Raiders tomorrow night. We have an open tryout from six to seven-thirty at the high-school field. You're a specialist. I think you might be a great specialist. No one will block your kicks, kid. You get them off faster than anybody I ever saw on TV."
Victor waited restlessly.
"If you make the team you get five dollars for every extra point, fifty bucks for every field goal. With me holding, we'll become damn famous, at least around here."
"You're not kidding?"
Champ saw his daughters climbing the fence and shouted for them to come on down and get home.
"Hey, Victor, I'm the president and you're part of my cabinet."

At the tryouts, Grupp selected most of his team. He found an adequate quarterback, Reed Chambers, whose most recent escapade had been a rape case, but Grupp had the charges reduced to simple assault and a fine, which Champ paid. Once Champ and Grupp saw Chambers' slick hand-offs and strong arm, they considered him a misunderstood young man. Victor was late, very late, for the tryouts. In fact, only Grupp and

THREE POINTS

Melvin were still around picking up loose helmets and balls. Grupp was ready to chew the kid out, but he saw Melvin's look of adoration. His own gaze drifted to the chunky, muscular legs, and he said instead, "Ok, let's see you do your stuff."

Victor pulled out his tee, grabbed a ball, and headed for the forty-yard line. Champ lunged after the boy.

The owner, dressed in white sports jacket and pink slacks, whined, "Victor, Victor, I'm your tee."

Grupp, through half-shut eyes, saw the Red Raiders' owner kneeling in the dirty portion of the grubby field as this Puerto Rican in a denim jacket, tight denim shorts, and Adidases didn't even try to kick the ball— and there it was splitting the uprights and laying docile in the end zone. Ten similar nonkicks and ten successful field goals resulting and Grupp started to lose his cool: That's Mr. Three Points, three damn points.

He then overhead Champ say loudly, "You don't have to worry about losing the ball, kick it into the stands if you want."

"What for, man? Why waste a good ball?"

Though Grupp was a great fool, he did a very smart thing. He ignored what he had heard and only remembered the end result—three points! He dubbed the Spic "Three Points," embraced his owner, then his new kicker. Finally it got so dark that there was nothing else for the three men to do except return to their respective residences.

Reed Chambers was tall, trim, with regular features and a moony look. He was the model of cliché heroes and was, of course, the lousiest of human beings. Hero in high school and downhill for the last five years, a nasty drunk and overly vicious bar-fighter and provoker. He worked at the local canning company and

THREE POINTS

was the star of their touch football and softball teams. But he was not the star of the Ripley Red Raiders. His passes were constantly dropped by receivers, and many times the throws were of the lame-duck variety. After a couple of games, his job was strictly maintenance man, handing off to his backs to get into range for three points by Cruz. Chambers hated that chump of a Spic with all his evil heart. Many a day Reed would stare at his arm and beseech it to throw straight, and then he would vilify the ends who seemed to be purposely missing or dodging the ball when it was thrown well. After three games Chambers had not passed for a touchdown and Cruz had kicked twelve field goals, while the defense, via interceptions and fumbles, had scored a couple of touchdowns. After three more games, Cruz's totals soared and Chambers's effectiveness stayed at the same zero level. Tall, whip-like, and decisive in his movements, he sure looked the picture of at least a semi-pro quarterback, but he was only spear carrier for Victor "Three Points" Cruz. Everyone was beginning to notice the amazing consistency and unbelievable kicking style of "Three Points." Chambers vowed revenge. He tried to get Victor into a fight, but Champ, for the first time living up to his name, chased the bully away, threatening a fine.

After eight weeks, the Raiders had won their division. They had scored six touchdowns (all by the defense) and thirty-one field goals out of thirty-one tries by the amazing out-of-work Puerto Rican. Finally Champ had an attraction: the championship game against the West Division winner, Hoboken Hornets, in two weeks at Ripley High School field. A crowd of five thousand was prophesied. The season could end up a financial and artistic success.

According to Champ's rules, Victor got fifty dollars

THREE POINTS

for each field goal and five dollars an extra point. Touchdowns were worth fifty dollars. A blocked kick was fifteen bucks, as was a fumble recovery. Grupp, who loved the game and loved to give orders, was paid nothing for his competent services. Chambers thus far had not made one cent and was truly foaming at the mouth.

Grupp decreed that a full scrimmage with pads would keep the team sharp during the two-week layoff before the championship game.

Chambers grabbed the coach by his sweat shirt.

"If I throw a pass for a t.d. in the scrimmage, will you give me fifty?"

Since Victor's kicking prowess had blossomed, José started to call his older brother "Vic Baby" and earnestly set out to prepare a proper scrapbook to record all of Vic Baby's exploits.

One night José said idly, "Boy, Poppa must be proud."

Victor's knees sagged and his eyeballs tilted.

"I practically forgot Poppa. I haven't seen him since . . ."

"Yeah, you never give us any more messages from him. But he must be around. He ain't left us ever."

Victor continued, "Since I started practicing in the park, he hasn't left one message. Damn!"

Felipe said, "I don't like it when he's not around. It makes us real orphans. At least with a ghost it was ok that just you saw him."

"You sure you ain't seen him, Vic Baby?"

"I'm damn sure," Victor snarled. "I hope."

"Even a ghost has to kick the bucket. What if Poppa really stays buried this time?" Felipe asked.

THREE POINTS

"Suppose you had two good arms," José teased.

"Ok, cut it," the older brother broke in. "But now I'm remembering things, things I should have noticed anyway."

"Like what?"

"Like a couple of times that motherfucker Champ Melvin fumbled the snap but the ball just stood straight and tall like a statue, and other times I could've sworn I didn't kick the ball right."

"Victor, you think . . ."

"Thinking is for the people who can afford problems."

"Just one more game, Vic Baby."

"And the scrimmage."

"You don't have to worry about a scrimmage."

But Victor was worrying plenty and groped about the apartment part of the night calling out to Poppa. But the ghost of Raymondo Cruz either wasn't around or wasn't answering, and Victor was so nervous that for the rest of the week he left notes everywhere begging his dead father to get in touch.

The afternoon of the scrimmage, Grupp approached Victor, who was shivering in the freezing dressing room. Many windows had been broken by vandals; not even the cold water worked in the shower. The only sounds were two toilets flushing and the smells of sweat and toilets backing up. Victor couldn't wait to get out on the field where it had to be warmer and more pleasant. He tried to pull away from Grupp's touch, but the coach held on.

"Take it slow today, Three Points. It's only a scrimmage."

"Ok, sure."

"Gotta save the best for the damn Hornets, right?"

THREE POINTS

"Ok. Let go, man, it's freezing."

"One thing, Champ has offered twenty bucks to each winning player in today's scrimmage."

"Heh, how can a defense win?"

"If they hold you under ten points in thirty minutes you lose."

"Jeez, I'll kick four field goals. Even that S.O.B. quarterback'll finally make a twenty."

"Uh, Chambers really wants fifty."

"So?"

"We don't want an unhappy quarterback for the big game. We don't want you kicking any field goals today."

"No? Why?"

"Here's a hundred from the prez. Just let Chambers have his fun today. Then boot 'em like hell next Sunday. Be compassionate today, Three Points. This is just between us. Maybe that mother will even throw a touchdown today. He's really had rotten luck. See ya, kid, and keep the hundred in your shoes. Remember, there's a lotta thieves on this squad."

A familiar voice cut through frigid silent air, "Don't worry Victor, your kicks will be true no matter what *they* want."

"Shit, it's been you all the time. Dumb of me not to think that out."

"You have a strong ego. I'm proud of you."

"It's been you all the time, every time."

"It's easy to guide the ball. I ride on it like it's a star going on a short trip."

"You're getting me in a bind, Poppa."

"You must always play to win. There is no other way. All great coaches say that."

"Grupp is no great coach."

"That's what I mean."

THREE POINTS

"Please."

"I love football. What a season we have shared."

"Have you been fucking up Chambers's passes?"

"Yes, I have been *deflecting* his passes," the ghost answered primly.

The lines collided and fought to a standstill. Every player wanted twenty bucks. It was their first chance for any kind of payday. Chambers was still looking for his first completion.

"Must be the wind," Grupp said on the bench. "His ball keeps rising and rising."

Victor shouted from the bench, "Keep trying, Reed old boy."

Chambers signaled time out and raced to the sideline.

"Don't you ever talk to me or ever say one dumb word to me. The hell with it," and he swung at Victor and missed. Only Victor heard the old ghost's cackle.

One of the offensive linesmen shouted, "Hey, put Three Points in. Let's go."

Three guys broke through the wedge and seemed about to envelop Victor and his bony holder, but it was as if a wire were suddenly yanked across the linesmen's charges as they fell. Victor nervously touched the ball with his little toe. *Three Points.*

And Chambers again had to be restrained.

Minutes later, another try for a field goal, and Grupp whispered, "Cut it out, Vic, miss the damn thing."

The ball was snapped high over everybody's head. Victor raced to pick up the loose ball. His knee caught it on a bounce, and it sailed high and handsome as usual, died the minute it passed the goal bar.

Alone on the bench, Victor said to a beaming Poppa,

THREE POINTS

"Let the prick pass in this game. Everybody should have some fun. Also, he's going to kill me one day, Poppa, when you're not around."

"Very well."

So Chambers stood in the pocket, fired angrily without much hope, and the receiver clutched the sixty-yard strike and stumbled into the end zone. Chambers looked beautiful; his face opened up into a beaming, toothful smile.

Chambers demanded no extra point. "Me and the Spic are tied."

"He cheated," Poppa whispered. "That's the only reason I let him complete it. You'd win with the extra point."

"Let him win, let him win. He's on our side."

Victor tried a field goal from the twenty, but the ball drifted wide and far to the left.

Champ hugged Victor, "You're a fine sportsman, Victor. You're quite a decent young man. Let's talk about a regular job after the season."

Poppa argued softly, "You're making a big mistake, my son."

Victor shifted restlessly in his bed, "Hey, it's my mistake then. It's my life. You gotta stay away from my foot during the game."

"You'll miss."

"Maybe, but I'm a good kicker. I won't miss all the time. It's important to me, Poppa."

The ghost was silent.

"And," Victor said firmly, "I want you to help Chambers this time. Let *him* be the fucking hero."

"Victor!" Poppa shouted.

"Poppa, I want to play without any help. Hey, I appreciate all you did this season. But it's enough."

They argued the rest of the night, but Victor would not yield.

The last pages of José's scrapbook completed the story.

HORNETS EDGE RED RAIDERS 26–24

Cruz fails as a rally led by brilliant Reed Chambers falls short. Quarterback Reed Chambers completed twenty of twenty-four passes for 375 yards and four scores, but a totally inept performance by Victor Cruz, who failed on all four extra points, and missed badly in six field goal attempts, left a valiant Raider team two points down. In an unbelievable turnabout in roles, Cruz was an extraordinary goat and Chambers heroic in a gallant exhibition under fire. Rumors abound that Chambers has been offered a contract to finish out the season with the Winnipeg Warriors of the Canadian Football League. Winnipeg has lost its two quarterbacks and has contacted the former Ripley High School great. This represents a great opportunity for the brilliant Chambers. Owner, Champ Melvin, was disconsolate at the heartbreaking loss and predicted massive changes in Raider personnel next season. "Another kicker is a definite possibility," he promised.

In the small park the ghost joined his son grimly pushing an empty swing.

"You failed to rob a bank, Poppa, and got gunned down for it. I just got canned and there goes the off-season job Melvin promised. Plus, he just warned me to stay out of the park."

"Don't worry, Chambers is going to fall worse than any of us. I goosed that ball every time he threw it. But those Canadians will smash him down to the size of a dwarf. And you didn't fail, Victor. You almost made one field goal."

"One woulda been enough."

"Victor, if you give it your all, you never fail. Every coach says that."

"Ok, Poppa."

"Football is too short a season."

"Thank God."

"Hey, you like when Chambers lost his pants?"

"Yeah, and he wasn't even wearing a cup! What a fool! The papers didn't mention *that*."

"Of course. But I shall miss football."

"Winning and losing are both unreal," Victor confessed.

"I truly loved the game. Some claim such sports help pass the time."

"It's for saps," Victor said slowly. "Nothing helps pass the time. Let's go home before Melvin calls the cops."

The ghost of Raymondo Cruz and his eldest son walked quickly, heads down, shoulders lowered. Right at that moment, it was a lovely late fall night, but you could get blind-sided at any second, and the two walked very close to one another.

Poppa advised needlessly, "From now on, Victor, sleep with one eye always open."

Caper

Mucho, sleeping like a horse, leaned against the door. Felipe and José tossed paper plates like Frisbees around the room as TVs, a radio, and the stereo squared off against each other. Through it all Victor sat in the far corner of the living room—a banished truant sucking his thumb. Victor realized it never did any damn good to read a dumb local newspaper story if what you read was already known, plucked off the grapevine buzz. All original hard news was being repeated on TV and the radio, and Victor knew all that gossip also.

So when a sixteen-year-old cheerleader is not raped or robbed, just definitely brain-crunched and left tied to a tree in a secluded swampy area near Sacred Home, everyone agreed here was a puzzling case. Plus scary. So Victor Cruz worried, but immediately concealed this emotion from himself. An ulcer now sprouted in Victor's guts, and he felt that if he could sweeten his sour body juices, then the ulcer would dissolve. The ghost of Raymondo Cruz could not understand Victor's inner pain.

"Never hide the worry," the ghost counseled his son, "or you will grow puffy with such worry and bust like some rotten pimple."

Victor had sneered, but it was a fake sneer that only revealed how the boy was keeping in his pain.

Poppa said gently, "Murders happen even in sweet suburbs. Even if there aren't uncollected garbage cans lying around, or winos, junkies, and muggers leaning on every street corner, someone always follows children and does them in. It happens."

"Ok, Poppa, ok!" Victor snapped.

"Why do you mourn at all? Did you know this girl or her loved ones?"

"The town always wanted Sacred Home closed down. Now they'll use the murder to get it done."

"The Church is still very tough," Poppa argued.

"The townies got clout, believe me. They never let Home kids go near their houses, even for Halloween, and if we stepped on their precious property, seconds later a cop was there to kick our butts. But we stole plenty from them anyway. But a murder is nowhere close to breaking and entering. They got the Home by the short hairs. Besides, the Church isn't that tough anymore, Poppa."

"Perhaps you worry needlessly."

"The swamp is our playground. Home kids who run away go there. Home kids who want to make it with some girl go there. If you wanna get high and if you got anything to sell or buy, you head to the 'patio.'"

"It's so close to Sacred Home?"

"Fuck, it's Home property."

"You hung out too?"

"Sure. Shit, you too, Poppa. We talked there a couple of times. It's very pretty in the spring before the weeds get too high, and the mosquitoes don't show until June."

"She might have been dumped in the swamp."

"What's the big difference? If somebody only dumped her, they can still blame it on us."

Poppa nodded.

Victor continued, "That dead chick went out with plenty Home dudes. She really dug Spics."

"That wasn't in the papers."

"Julio is mop boy in Burger & Donut World. I seen him two days ago. Word of mouth beats crap outta any newspaper. Julio told me all the heavy stuff . . ."

"Such as?" Poppa coughed nervously.

"She was dumb like us. She was in D-track in high school. She went down with a dozen or more, and she took guys like us to her home for supper and into her bedroom."

"What'd her folks say?"

"Mother is a manicurist, father is in construction. What do you think they said?"

"None of this sounds good."

"Hey, they're howling and blaming the whole Rican nation. But we gotta go over and maybe find something out. Sacred Home is in more trouble than us. Imagine."

"Victor, they'll suspect you."

"They want it to be us, like sharks that need blood for their kicks. They'll even frame us, but they probably won't have to, the rotten fucks."

"If you're seen prowling, the police will pick you up."

"They already questioned me."

"When?"

"Today."

"They third-degreed you, my son?"

"Just routine. They're asking every ex-Home kid who's still around the county."

"They question Felipe?"

"Yeah, but Felipe's got a great alibi. He was working. Lucky for him, since he's a terrific suspect."

"Hold your tongue."

"Anyway, we're all innocent. Now we gotta find out who did it."

"And then?"

"Hope for a miracle."

"What was the girl's name?"

"Mary."

Poppa nodded, pretending to be a wise judge. However, the more he nodded, the more woozy he became. Finally Poppa dozed off as Victor meditated and hoped to somehow heal his throbbing ulcer.

After supper the brothers leaned into a huddle.

"I bet there are more cops than nuns at Sacred Home."

"We shouldn't go."

"We owe it," Victor stated decisively.

Felipe challenged brusquely, "To who?"

"Yeah," José parroted.

"We can't be that lucky. The Home helped."

José strutted about, "It helped throw me out of school and sicced dogs on me when I showed up last year."

"If a Home guy did it, it's curtains for the joint."

Felipe said, "Shit, anybody coulda done it. The Ignazio brothers warned her to only lay for Guineas. They mighta tried to scare her and got carried away."

José now pamphleteered, "It's a political crime, yeah,

political because in this society you gotta mug, exploit, and murder. Look at history, man."

Felipe bellowed, "Look at what? You jerk!"

Victor argued, "We got this far. So Sacred Home helped. Don't fuckin' ask me how, but it did."

Suddenly Felipe lost interest in rebelling. Conversation always tired him.

"Talk is cheap. We'll go if you want."

"I wanna see Sister Noreen shaky and taking pills."

"Sister taking uppers?"

"Downers, stupido."

Victor bossed, "Felipe, go call us a taxi."

The ghost of Raymondo Cruz zipped up his shabby windbreaker and followed Felipe downstairs. Mucho, never eager to go out at night, hid under the couch. Poppa lay on the taxi roof as if it was some private beach. Victor smirked.

The taxi driver was angry.

"Where you guys going?"

"Sacred Home."

"That's ten dollars."

"So?"

"I'm just telling you the rates, so you know."

José stood alongside Felipe and spat out sharply, "Ok, just so you just don't think you can charge us by weight. We don't want no political taxi rides."

Felipe roared with laughter and a noisy, giggling trio plopped into the cab. On the way they bullied down the price to five bucks, and José, delighting in the role of gentle bully, informed the frightened driver, "And for that price we don't cut off your ears."

Poppa, still moonbathing on the roof, smiled and smiled—how could you not admire such children.

The next morning, Victor was aware of being tailed as he dodged traffic on the busy highway and headed for the Roadside Diner. The food was lousy, but its owner frequently hired Felipe and José as dishwashers during busy weekends. Victor, the wily solid American citizen, dined at the Roadside daily so his brothers would get first call when the need for second-rate help arose. The owner greeted Victor by first name. Victor only hoped the lousy food wouldn't encourage his damn ulcer.

On the way to the diner, Victor had smelled cop inside the unmarked car and its dumb snail's pace alongside him, so he was not surprised one little bit when a fat, pleasant-featured man sat down at his table just as the pork chops, baked beans, and orange soda appeared.

"You know who I am?" the guy asked.

"Cop."

"Plainclothes," he answered proudly.

Victor grappled with the tough-skinned chops.

"Sister Noreen said you visited her last night and said you wanted to help out the Home."

"That's right, man. And my brothers feel the same. We already been questioned."

"Did I ever bust you?"

"I don't think so."

"Me neither. But I got a bad memory. I checked on you. You're pretty clean, so I'm giving you some advice."

"I like advice."

The man had very weird eyes, the left one a glazed blue that seemed looking for faraway things. The right eye was smaller, irritated, twitchy, and ferocious. There was an intensity that could bore a hole in you. Strange guy, Victor decided right away.

138

"Don't hang around the Home or the swamp again. There's vigilante groups riding shotgun all over the area just looking for an excuse to be a posse. Tell you what, though. Whenever you hear something, anything, call me. Here's my card."

Scribbled on a wrinkled, stained postcard:

> Lester Boidelman
> Office of the District Attorney
> 358-8906 twenty-four hours on call

Victor was about to give up on his pork chops. His stomach was really getting oily.

"Wow, you got a card like a salesman."

Boidelman replied pompously, "I *am* a salesman, kid. I sell the idea of keeping your nose clean. You never heard of me in your crowd?"

"Nope."

"I'm the poet cop."

"Sorry."

"I know a lot of your graduating class."

"Ah, they don't read poetry."

Boidelman grinned boyishly. "That's why I'm a cop. But my first love was poetry. Have you read Lorca in school?"

"Lorca?"

"They should have Spanish studies in the high school. I'd vote for it in a school bond issue. Look, I'll send you a copy and we'll talk about it one time."

Victor ordered milk.

Boidelman continued, "When I was your age, Victor, all I wanted to be was a great poet. But I didn't like the idea of not eating. And besides, I already saw that I didn't have much talent. Didn't want to be town cop forever, so I got into undercover work."

Victor didn't point out that the cop had forgotten his tie, at least for today. Instead the boy drank greedily, soothing his aching ulcer. Boidelman offered an after-dinner peppermint and Victor accepted.

"I'm no hypocrite. I smoke grass myself and I look the other way in the Mall and other places kids are turning on. I just want you to believe I can be trusted. I never make cheap arrests, and therefore my superiors dislike me and my peers detest me. I don't give a shit. I just want to nail the murderer of Mary O'Hara. See, murder is clear and simple: you get who did it and then there is a restoring of balance."

Victor ad libbed, "Yeah, an eye for an eye."

"Right. Look, I'm going to send you those poems anyway."

"If we hear anything about the murder, we'll pass it on."

"Any rumor will do, Victor. You want to hear a beauty. Yesterday, we get a call from a lady. Some guy forced her off the road, pulled her out of the car, and took her into the bushes. He does a really heavy number and dresses her, throws her back in her car, and warns her to keep her mouth shut."

Victor waited patiently.

"I asked her if she could give a description of the assailant, and she said it was President Ronald Reagan in a souped-up Chevy, looking for action."

Victor laughed. "You sure you want to hear all the rumors?"

"I'd appreciate it. If I don't make a name for myself, there's a terrific chance of being slapped back down to uniformed cop again."

Victor looked at him sadly.

"I'm telling you from the heart, kid. I still like writing bad poetry, but I also love wearing a suit and carrying my gun."

Victor spotted some meat inside the cracked bone of the pork chop.

"Can you pass the ketchup?"

In the sunny kitchen, the brothers were drinking coffee with plenty of milk and sugar. Victor passed around a bowl of M&Ms.

"Estrella never answered my card."

"She can't read English, Victor."

"You got to go in tomorrow morning and get her, José."

José was still the only Cruz eager to make the trek back to the bleak Bronx and visit crazy Momma and the other freaks, like Estrella the gypsy hooker, who was usually out of work in both her chosen fields.

Felipe sneered, "Easy to find that one. She'll be at the social club hustling drinks and cocks."

Victor agreed. "I'll call Mr. Boidelman and we'll meet you at the bus stop at twelve o'clock."

José shrugged, "Ok, ok, but I don't like cops, even nutty cops."

"Did you read the poetry, José?"

"Nah."

Felipe asked, "Since when you got all this respect for Estrella, Victor?"

"In this kind of trouble she might feel at home and figure out who killed the girl."

The ghost of Raymondo Cruz accepted full credit for the decision to invite the gypsy to do a reading at the murder scene. Mucho, the awkward one, had just returned from the vet minus three benign tumors and costing a hundred big ones, so there was a need for money in every dusty niche of the apartment. They could just about make the rent this month. Utilities and the vet bill munched off Victor's wounded ulcer.

"The reward, the reward," Poppa hissed at Victor.

"Hey Felipe," Victor shouted. "How much is the reward?"

"Two hundred," José answered. "It would be beautiful if the Rotary Club had to pay us."

Felipe spat out, "Aah, kids are worth nothing in the open market. You hear on ABC radio how this couple sold their kid to a farmer for three chickens."

Now it was Raymondo Cruz's stomach in torment. He saw that Victor's sensitivity came from him and the ghost's despair deepened.

José, up early, made a lot of noise in the kitchen before heading for the Bronx. When Boidelman drove by later in the morning, Felipe and Victor were already sitting on the stoop waiting.

Boidelman smiled, "Hey, you guys are early."

"You too," Victor pointed out.

It only took a few minutes to drive to the bus stop in front of the boarded-up A&P. Across the street was a bankrupt Fish & Chips and a weed-littered lot. Only a discount liquor store halfway down the block was open.

"You sure the bus even comes by here?" Victor asked. The sunny morning got much hotter. Boidelman stretched out and read the *New York Times*; Felipe and Victor fiddled with the car radio until they found a hard-rock station. A couple of boring hours passed; three city buses had come and gone and still no José and Estrella. Boidelman remained calm and very patient. The fourth bus arrived and out poured Estrella.

Behind her José carried an Alexander's shopping bag. Estrella was not happy.

"Here she is, chief."

"Lester Boidelman, ma'am. Are you ready?"

"Yeah, you the cop?"

"Yes. I mean, can't you tell?"

"I just got here. I don't like doing murders. Suppose this girl deserved it? Suppose one of them," she pointed at the brothers, "did it?"

The brothers giggled nervously. The cop saw the Lorca book in José's jacket.

"Hey, you read the book, José?"

"Sure," José lied.

"What do you think?"

"Terrific stuff."

"That's what I think, too."

"Can I drive us to the swamp, Mr. Boidelman?" Felipe asked. Boidelman nodded.

Once they reached the swamp, Felipe parked under a bent tree and Estrella waited in the car until Boidelman's wirecutter tore away the makeshift barbed-wire fence. The swamp smelled like ageless rot.

"Wow, it's not a patio anymore. What an odor! What is it?"

"Sewer line broke a few days ago."

"Jeez, smells like hell."

"Looks like hell," Estrella said. "You boys are never going to grow up."

Boidelman confessed, "I'm willing to try anything."

Estrella misunderstood and smiled provocatively. Victor elbowed the gypsy's butt.

"Rub your crystal balls, not his, Estrella."

José planted down the shopping bag. The gypsy gracefully reached in and pulled out two empty goldfish bowls. She spat in one and rubbed it across her chest and spat again. She flung the bowl away. She started loving up the second bowl. Felipe got an erection. The others looked away. Boidelman no longer appeared tranquil. The gypsy's finger was bleeding, and she did a split, the equal of any goalie, as she pressed the goldfish bowl between her legs under her dress, then raised it to her left ear and then to her eyes and back to her right ear.

She squeaked, "Where was the girl's body found, where?"

Boidelman pointed.

"I see white people carrying a body."

"Yahoo!" José shouted.

Felipe said, "Those goddamn Ignazios done it."

Victor felt a sense of relief and patted his throbbing stomach.

Estrella had forgotten them. She sat demurely on the ground as if expecting a picnic. Boidelman joined her and she started an unrhythmic chant.

"They killed her at home, in the den, and then they brought her here, tied her up. I don't see faces, but I see and hear names."

"What names, what names?" the cop asked.

"Ella."

"Shit," José snapped, "her goddamn name was Mary."

Boidelman said curtly, "The mother's name is Ella."

Estrella shouted, "The other name is Charley."

"The father," Boidelman answered her.

Estrella summed up, "They dumped her here to frame the Home."

The cop gallantly helped her up.

"I'll drive you home, Miss."

On the way back, Boidelman said, "We'll have to lay a trap. But I can't figure out what kind of trap."

CAPER

"When you gave her the fifty, didn't you hear Estrella say she'd lay a hex on them?"

"Frankly, we can't rely on that either." The cop sounded tired and looked real old, both eyes now had that faraway look.

"If something does happen one day, the reward is yours, even if it has to come out of my pocket. But right now, it's still a dead-end caper."

Victor said hopefully, "Maybe something will happen. When Estrella is hot, she's hot."

Three days later, the parents of Mary O'Hara drove off a nearby bridge and left a suicide note and confession, which the local paper printed.

> Our daughter was pregnant and we could no longer bear the shame of what she did to us and now we cannot bear what we did to her. We hope to be forgiven some day.

A few days later, the brothers received a fifty-dollar bill without a note. During the next few weeks more envelopes with bills of lesser denominations arrived. The utility bill and the vet were paid off. Then one day a letter was delivered without any money inside.

> Dear Boys:
> I been sending you the reward in bits and pieces. My superiors wouldn't allow you to win the money and the Rotary people withdrew their offer. Of course, nobody believed my story and I didn't tell them half, believe me.
> We also lost the election and right now I'm out of a job. There's a small town upstate that answered my resumé. It's for a postman/sheriff and for pretty good money considering. It would be a swell place to live and write, so I guess I'll take the offer. I still owe you a hun-

dred, and you will get it, but slowly. I'm sure you will understand.

Well, it was nice working with you all. We have served Lady Justice well and I am only sorry I didn't get to talk to Jose more about the poetry. When I find another good book, I will send it along. Nice meeting you.

The boys agreed to put the Lorca book on their prize coffee table alongside *Penthouse* and *Playboy*. And it stayed there for many months. Only the ghost of Raymondo Cruz was curious enough to really try reading it, and he quickly gave up.

Rappin' with Felicia

Felicia stood at the door and waited for José to open. But he wouldn't let her in, though he was aware that she was waiting. Finally she knocked softly. Sighing, she knocked louder. Still José hadn't moved. Felicia got a little nervous, as usual, and knocked and kicked at the door. Then José, smiling like a cat after the big goldfish dinner, opened the door and impatiently motioned her inside.

It could be the grass, but the apartment looked bigger, much bigger, Felicia observed after a lengthy silence.

"Maybe you're right."

"Hey, it can't be bigger."

"Maybe your eyes got much smaller."

José wondered what time it was exactly. His brothers had gone to a double feature, probably'd be stopping off at a bar before they finally got back. He definitely wanted Felicia out before they returned. Nobody was actively competitive about most things, but a lead in make-out standings could always be a tender point, and

Felipe and Victor might very well tumble Felicia just for the hell of it. Plus, of course, Felicia just never said no. Still, José knew she would be happier not doing it, and José also knew Felicia was embarrassed having him see her elephant legs pressuring some other dude's shoulders. She had a tough life because she was fat and usually looked sad and moony. Also, Felicia's life was even tougher since the girl absolutely lacked imagination. José regularly infused her life with creative doses and Felicia loved him for his trouble. And he was glad she had gained all her massive weight back.

The quicksilver thing that made the relationship between José and Felicia something more than an inevitable wrestling match was that sometimes neither of them tried to hide between each other's legs and grunts. They didn't kid themselves one damn bit on those occasions: they just lay around, smoked joints, and José talked and talked—and for Felicia it was more than good. Clearly she didn't care if they ever made love, as long as the boy hung around. And José didn't know for sure why he allotted so much time to this blubbery piece when so many chicks really dug him and he could convince any woman to stay around for a night. However, José enjoyed seeing his confessions, doubts, and bravado bounce off Felicia's head.

José sat on her lap, his small handsome face cradled between her sticky boobs. He instinctively mouthed a massive teat and hung on, choking happily. Felicia struggled to keep her hands still; if she began even stroking his afro, they'd have to yield this rap time. And she loved to hear José wail out like some strange Puerto Rican philosopher. If only he'd finish high school, take his equivalency test, there'd be no stopping him. He was such a deep, bottomless person. She finally rested her chubby, agitated hands alongside the boy's narrow thighs, but she was very careful to avoid brushing his nuts.

"You going to tell a story."

"Sure I am, and it ain't Mother Goose."

"Don't be dirty."

"The story is called Marc the Narc."

"I don't wanna hear it, please."

"Hey, the names have been changed so nobody gets pissed, but my story is real and has a moral."

"Moral is exactly what?"

"What teaches you something. See you can learn from a clown who makes it or loses."

"Sometimes you talk like a college kid."

Soon as Felicia had entered the apartment, she went topless. Then it was up to the two participants what kind of action would develop. Her breasts ballooned and expanded and filled yards of empty space; she saw his crotch about to explode. Felicia tried not to move at all.

"Let's have the story first."

"No."

"C'mon, José."

"Play while I talk."

"Then you'll forget the story. Just screw me."

"Bitch, you say it like I'm a menace."

"Say what then?"

"Shit, say fuck."

"You'll fuck me, and I wanna hear the story about the narc, Nick Romero."

"Hey, Nick was his real name. But in my story, Felicia, it's Marc."

"Shit, José, if you mean Nick Romero, just say it."

"I ain't saying his name again all night. You best never remember the story with his name in it."

"C'mon, don't get pissed."

Sullenly, he took out his dick. Felicia sighed, reached

over, and held on. They watched, fascinated, as his dick expanded considerably. Felicia whistled seriously.

"You got a masterpiece."

He replied, "Don't let go. It's never been as big as this!"

Then he continued his tale.

"Marc was a bully all his life, built tough and very good with his fists when he was challenged. He was one bad dude, a bully, and a rat. He saw right away how to get ahead was to rat on your friends. If you tell nuns and cops all the action that's going on and is planned, you yourself can get away with murder and are rewarded while you listen to your pals howling as they get worked over. When Marc was little they called him rat, shit, and squealer, but only when he got past eighteen and hung in the streets and the bars was he not just a crummy tattletale anymore, but a full-time narc, a goddamned informer."

"Should be wiped out."

"Aah, he was Puerto Rican. There was hope for him to straighten out and be a regular guy; only we knew it would probably never happen. Meanwhile, plenty of good guys, real brothers, were being nailed. Marc was getting to be one terrific pain in everyone's ass. Then he got lucky, and we thought now he'd lay off."

"Somebody finally broke his arms and legs."

"No."

"You and your brothers didn't get into it?"

"Hey, this is like *Love Story*."

"If you're involved, José, I'm going to faint."

"Just swing my thing. Look, it's dropping off to sleep."

"Do you have a tissue?"

"You are my tissue."

"That's not comical."

"Won't you be my tissue?"
"You know I'd do anything for you."
"Just keep my dick alive. That's all I'm requesting."
"Ok, now finish the story."
"Yeah, good, not too fast. Perfect. That is really perfect, my dear Felicia.

"Then Marc got so lucky a blind man could cry. Some white lady, divorced or widowed, about thirty-five, tanned and plenty rich, really dug Marc. She lived in a mansion with a couple of her kids and a few maids. So now Marc lay with a blonde heiress. She was his maid. Shit, he could go around the world every year."

She giggled.

"Traveled, traveled around the world. Donkey!"

"José, you're going to come soon. Take it easy."

"Don't worry, if it's one thing I got it's control. See Marc had to be a dick. He couldn't stop ratting on our little numbers game, the little hustling, the small-time soft drug deals. All the little pleasures that make life pay off in small change. See, cops have to nail small potatoes. That way they don't feel so guilty taking Mafia payoffs on big stuff. And with a guy like Marc seeing and hearing everything and spending part of his life in a phone booth, the county jails kept filled."

Nervously, she leaned harder against him.

"Swell. Like I said before, I got mugged. They all knew Marc was no fucking good, so everybody tried to be cool and just talk bullshit when he came around, but you know guys get excited and they blow what's happening. Marc was buying beer for everybody since he not only got paid off by the cops, but his lady stuffed his pockets with cash. So, in some ways, he's fun to be around, but he's also dangerous as hell, because by now most guys in the bar have given up and grown up, and are thinking hard on some racket. Even new ways to beat welfare. One night Marc flashes a really extra big roll and this dude—let's call him Tom—gets envious and says the woman must be easily satisfied if she lays such cash bundles on a mutt cock. Marc goes ape, punches the guy on the nose, immediately drawing a little blood. That was a very big error on his part, since Tom is a real bar fighter who immediately breaks a Bud on the counter and shoves the biggest bottle chunk up his chest. Buckets of blood pour out and Marc right away turns three shades lighter and he's positively dying when he hits the sawdust floor. The cops show and there's this crazy scene. As he dies, Marc gives the name of his killer, Tom's alias, and names every racket Tom has ever done. Then Marc looks carefully at all of us huddling in the bar. He calls us by name, and shit, rattles off everything we ever done illegal since we were kids, even Halloween pranks. The cops are in tears over such spunk and they are writing it down faster than he is squealing, but Marc dies before he can sign his name, so they got no one to arrest but Tom."

"So Nick is dead. Nick Romero is dead."

"Here I come!" José shouted happily. "Let her rip."

"Jeez, it's all over me. It's everywhere. What a blast."

"I never kid around."

She got a towel and wiped him, then herself, and finally asked, "What's the moral?"

"You have to diversify."

"Explain."

"You have to have more than one interest. You can't be one person, play one game."

"Why not?"

"I'm a triple agent," he boasted.

"Is that good?" she worried.

"It saved my life."

"How, José?"

"First, I wanted to blow buildings and people up, change society real fast. Hell, the FBI woulda gunned me down pretty fast also. Then I didn't want to do any drastic stuff and worked three jobs a day, you remember that. Shit, I woulda had an ulcer in a year if I only walked the straight and narrow."

"Yeah, I can understand," Felicia smiled shyly.

"Now I have one straight job. I do a little grass, hustle, and I'm beginning to think revolution again. Only this time I'm keeping it secret from everybody. It's fuckin' hard to be a triple agent."

"And that's good," she repeated.

"When I die and when I live I don't want to be all neat and tidied up like Nick was or anybody else. I want lots of interests and things spinning."

"You'd never be a narc."

"Stupid! What I'm saying is I need dreams at night and lots of real things going when I'm not sleeping. Dig?"

"Maybe."

He studied her. Felicia's boobs dangled limply to the floor. He studied himself. His dick had retired for the evening. They were now both naked before each other, but neither was aroused. She snuggled against him and he snuggled back. Then he became an informer and ratted on Felicia—fat, dopey, an unbelievable jelly body and an ass like a sofa. And he informed on himself: I am not always a con man and triple agent. I like leaning on her and her leaning back. He tried to cover them both with the garish yellow-and-red bathtowel. Scribbled across the center of the terry cloth in loose thread was CONEY ISLAND, USA.

When Felipe and Victor finally staggered home, they discovered José and Felicia sound asleep in each other's arms. The towel had skittered to the floor and lay alongside an empty wine bottle. The room smelled very pleasantly of come, grass, wine, and human sweat. Victor and Felipe giggled softly, saw the two figures as hazy, unborn children. So the brothers tiptoed off to sleep.

Victor's Damn Luck

"José is the big rapper of our tribe. Wow, that kid bulls even in his sleep. Big mugger Felipe will mumble aloud once in a while, so it's just me that hides thoughts and other stuff inside. The kind of jerk who gets his ulcer bleeding because all these things skip around in my gut while my mouth stays tight as a damn clam. I tried writing a history of my family, but that's still not talking. Writing is still thinking quietly about the mess, then scribbling crap out on paper. José finally fixed the tape recorder, and I'm back in business. So it's more than funny me standing here like an announcer or M.C. yakking straight out like this and hearing my tape play back. My voice is a funny dumb squeaking sound, like my shadow was talking.

"I stopped writing the Cruz history because plenty was happening right now and I got fouled up in all the action, so the past meant shit. I'll probably remember highlights in a few months. And begin writing again. The hardest part about writing was memorizing and learning all the new words I needed. Words are like all shapes and sizes of balls that you can kick, throw, or volley around. Kind of fun, but you gotta have plenty of spare time to write.

"Also, I got one hard-mother job. I open this small Mobil garage on the busiest traffic spot in the county. I got to walk to the damn place more than a fucking mile before six o'clock every damn weekday morning. For the next three hours I handle plenty of money. We don't accept credit cards, and I open and close that register all day. Can you really understand the pressure of not copping one cent?

"The only sad thing about the good guy who owns the garage is that he's old. He lost his wife last year and he's not too healthy himself. They never had kids, and he ain't in any mood to get it up early in the morning, pump gasoline, repair cars, and keep smiling at customers. So me, Victor Cruz, pumps gas, repairs busted cars, and smiles at everybody like it was a holiday, and I'm working my ass off. Oh, I get the damn luck. I got the job of being very honest every damn day. Being Mr. Clean puts me in the sauna sweats though it's less than ten degrees outside. Receipts work out perfect every day, and I ain't asked José to give me any ideas for clever rip-offs, but the little punk keeps hinting he's got a few plans. I'm under weird pressure, like you know that streamroller in old cartoons that creams some nutty dog or cat into a flat pancake. When I get back home I eat like a tired bird and only listen to TV, because I'm too tired to open my eyes.

"I got to speak a little more about luck. My damn luck. For I am easily the luckiest of the Cruz brothers. The latest example, not counting the garage job, is we all banged the same runaway chick and only me didn't get a dose. José and Felipe were sore as hell, but they come to expect it. Victor's damn luck. And only I smile.

"Like two weeks ago when we found this guy passed out in front of the house. He's dressed ok, not bummy, but we'da passed him by except it was pouring. So we lugged the old geezer upstairs. First thing we see is that he's not drunk, but really shaking, so he's either sick or dying. Felipe is all for tossing him out a window and forgetting the whole bit. José would like to rifle the dude's overcoat and pants pockets. But I stiff-armed both of 'em and called an ambulance. Couple of days later the old guy is alive and well and visits us. He brings along a carton of McDonalds best—plenty of Big Macs, Quarter Pounders, fries, apple crisps, Coke, shakes, also two six-packs of beer and a big box of candy. Plus he introduces himself and thanks us for helping him out. He's Mike Donovan—he's a diabetic—and when we found him, he was into some sugar shock. Shit, he can't thank us enough because he is not ready to die just yet—he's got plenty of moxie. You know Donovan reminds me of the old lady we worked for last year. Only Mrs. Malloy, she was ready to die when she hired us. She had us tidy up her mansion for the mourners—I just figured that one out.

"Anyway, Donovan tells us we can choose to see who will hire on as his helper at the garage. The last guy just quit and Donovan needs an experienced man. Pay is $200 a week. You gotta open the joint and work till four in the afternoon, when he closes for the day. Years and years, Donovan and his old lady worked hours like a candy store, but now with her dead and him almost there, where's the reason to keep open twenty-four hours? Donovan very definitely can't run a busy station anymore, and my damn luck, don't you see, is I qualified. Hell, I worked in a body shop and can do beautiful work for a cheap and fair price. Only I'm healthy and able. José don't want to get a fingernail dirty and, besides, he's unreliable. Felipe is bigger than

Godzilla, but let's face it, for heavy, demanding work and having to squirm from car to car, he's got only one very outstanding working arm. So it's only me. I like being dirty, goosing under cars, gassing them up, and I really dig bending fronts and fenders back into shape. Hey, ok, I dig the whole garage scene, but I could use help running Donovan's joint. He's a tight-fisted Mick, but also very nice and straight. No matter how you slice it, it's only me alone sweating my nuts off and being fucking honest every damn day. That's my luck sure and simple. You can hear Felipe and José howling in the next room. They're watching 'Bowling for Dollars,' watching dummies bowl, trying to score two strikes. And me, the lucky Cruz, sits in the coldest room in our apartment, alone with a dumb machine.

"Another reason I really love the garage is what's behind the Mobil station. A goddamn palace of a junkyard. Everything in the world is there from spare car parts, to beds, to silverware, and furniture. Picture frames and, of course, garbage. Poppa is always hanging around the junkyard. He pointed out that a junkyard is where, if you're smart, you only grab what's good from the pile and stay away from loser items and rotten smells. Poppa says you should do that with life, have a second and third chance, and make only smart moves.

"We've come up with a terrific old dresser. Felipe stripped it down to its original looks. We had to carry that dresser two miles back to our place. We stuck it in the foyer with nothing in it. Still has nothing in it, but it looks special and important. Classy! We also found a couple of not-bald snow tires, a mess of TVs that might work, a few chipped but ok salad bowls and platters, and plenty of knives and forks. Right now we're looking for lamps and small tables. They got plenty, but not what we want. See, we're picky and patient. In a few days, tons of new junk will be there. And there are always more winners than losers in the yard, and it's open to everybody.

"Boy, you should see how Poppa really digs that junkyard! He told me he has lunch there on any day it's not too windy. If that little man was alive, I know what we'd give him for all the Father's Days he missed—a pocketful of cash and a great auction where he could bid on shit and workers would carry his 'Sold' items to where he lived and Poppa would sit there in the crowd bidding and bidding until his heart burst."

"Andy Kousitsky's a Russian, but he could be a Jew. Believe me, he only knows deals. The guy is incredible, calls himself the poor prince Andrei Kousitsky. But after a beer or glass of wine or Coke or Ritz cracker, as long as it's free, he'll say call him Andy, and right away tries to pull some fast one, some kind of deal. He's been over all week, even brought along bagels with him. Only he really has something to peddle this time. Kousitsky claimed that he admired us, particularly me, because we pay rent right on the first of the month and keep the apartment clean, and keep the outside neat, too. Not because we're janitors, but because we like it clean. And, shit, who doesn't know no landlord will shovel snow or sweep away sidewalk dirt.

"This is the deal he offered. We should take over the downstairs store, fix it up into an antique shop. Kousitsky looked around our apartment and said, 'You boys are into fag stuff anyway and there's money in it. Big money!' We buy our apartment for a few bucks more a month, and we'll be condominium owners and he'll toss in the top floor which we can use for private junkyard storage. What worried me most of all was it sounded like a wonderful idea. Poppa was not clicking his tongue reminding me nobody helps out Puerto Ricans, including other Puerto Ricans. José could be the smooth used-furniture salesman conning customers. Felipe is superfast finding the original finish and Poppa happily snorts stripping fluid like it's horse. And with the junkyard less than two miles away, we got ourselves a big reliable source. If Kousitsky puts us onto a cheap pickup truck, we may be in big business.

"Once, years ago, we dreamed we'd all run a bodega, but cancel that; that's nickels and dimes and rotten hours. Then later we thought about opening a social club with dice and card games, some girls, and a small bar. But shit, even in a dream that meant paying off cops and there would always be trouble late at night. Antiques is a soft, white business, but all three of us do have respect for very old, well-made stuff. We don't know shit about antiques. Kousitsky says nobody else does either, so we're even. He promised us a write-up in the local paper. Kousitsky's personal angle is he owns most of the buildings on our death valley street, so if we can work out to be a success, then other antique shops will open and all the customers and sucker crowds will make it 'Main Street.' Therefore he sounded pretty sincere.

"'You kids sometimes work like beavers, but the money you earn is peanuts. This time with Kousitsky helping, you will see hard and heavy cash. I need you, you need me. We are almost partners.'"

"Next, Donovan got into the picture, sold me his pickup truck real cheap. I can pay it off easy in a few months. With all the lousy weather, we got a boatload of busted cars to fix and I get a cut of each big job. Donovan is one sweet guy, 'You can have all the antiques in my attic, Victor. I know there's a couple of Tiffany lamps up there. Hell, kid, you can have me. I'm a priceless relic.'

"Things look good. I mean good. Poppa has been so happy lately, he hasn't complained about how the wind rattles through the bullet holes in his body. Every winter he complains, and this has been a real cold, windy couple of weeks, but he's too busy to notice. Just like us."

"Well, there are nice things happening. If you lean out our living room windows at night, you could see our store sign lights sliding off the snow piled in the gutter: THE CRUZ SHOP OF BARGAINS GALORE. Felipe and José painted the sign. Kousitsky donated the lights, and for another surprise he had one hundred business cards printed.

"Opening night was a smash! We had all kinds of free food: Russian glop, a big pail of red soup, and hundreds of pancakes all filled with sour cream, platters of Jewish deli, three pots of chicken, and rice and beans. Donovan made a giant corned beef and cabbage and we have twenty bags of all kinds of potato chips and pretzels and tons of wine and beer and soda. Plenty of strangers and our friends showed, like Donovan, Kousitsky, fat Felicia and her juicy buddies from around the corner, and people from the newspaper. With all those people there was fun, but no loud noise. So it was the most sophisticated party we were ever at. Believe me, and it wasn't hard picking up after they left. They weren't real slobs. But as I'm looking up, Poppa was gloomy again, complaining about the bullet holes. Shit. He said there should be noisy young children running around at good family parties.

"'But there are no children! Where are my little

Cruzes? Where are my grandchildren?' He wailed and pointed out how the wind tearing open the bullet-hole scabs made his wounds much wider and infected all over again. Double shit."

"Even though the store started selling out like we only stocked brand-new hot merchandise, I was feeling lousy because Poppa can be a downer experience. Even when three Tiffany lamps Donovan gave us were sold to one customer for enough to pay rent for three months, I still couldn't sleep good. The next two weeks I was up walking around at night as much as Poppa. Finally, one night, I'm so conked some of my bones were already snoring when I heard jimmying at the store door. Now who the fuck ever heard of antique thieves? That's like stealing stiffs from the graveyard. I woke up my brothers, we sneak downstairs and grab the bandit. Only it wasn't a bandit or a junkie, not a midget or a kid exactly. It was a small person who looked like the three of us. No shit, it's crazy, but fuckin' true. He's got Felipe's broad shoulders and wide chest, there's José's sweet eyes, and he has my pigeon-toed walk, my nose, and my small ears. The little person doesn't know how old he is. He doesn't care either. He's real small for his age, which is about twelve, we figure. He was smoking a smelly thin cigar when we rushed him and he kept cursing us out and saying, 'Momma sent me! Get the fuck off!' Seems she threw him out of the house. Told him what county we were in and this small person has been looking for us for a couple of weeks. 'I'm a Cruz, you fucks. I'm a fucking Cruz,' he kept shouting.

"Maybe it's true, but our Poppa making it with his crazy wife is not on the small list of miracles a Puerto

Rican ghost can pull off. Ok then, by some voodoo magic the small person popped out of Momma, smoking a cigar and cursing better than anybody. I mean, you can get dizzy how he looks exactly like all of us. He's crazy as hell, and is going to mean trouble, but we decided to keep him. Finally, the small person says his name is Jeremiah Cruz.

"Glad this tape is running out. I got one sore throat."

"Fuck you, Victor and the others. Some shitty brothers. I'm not going to any dumb junior high school. I ain't going. What are you, nuts? You fucks, packing me a lunch, giving me pencils and notebooks like I'm a fag. You love school so much, you go to junior high. Listen good. I'm full of ideas, but school *ain't* one of them. I'll never be a jive-ass lawyer—nothing like that. You guys are really retarded. Nuts! Fuck you."

"The punk locked himself in the bathroom and is smoking a cigar and cursing us out. He's got to come out some time, and then Felipe will walk him to school every morning and José can find out when the small person plays truant. They will report when I get back from the garage, then I'll stomp him good. But he's going to play ball. One thing about small person, he's smart. The school guidance was in shock when they saw his IQ was higher than any white kid's. I know we'll be able to bribe him. Smart people have a price too. Just think of a Cruz bailing out his brothers one day or helping us screw Kousitsky legally. Poppa was right, too: it *is* better to have a kid around, more fun than our three-legged dog. 'See, see, kids make for

163

happy occasions and endings,' Poppa said when he first spied small person. 'You know, like the hero riding his horse into the sunset.'"

"A few days ago José got very nervous and started stuttering again, 'Hey, it's all going to change, ain't it. We gotta mess up soon, r-r-r-right?'
"'Is today great?' I asked.
"'Yeah, why?'
"'Was yesterday very good?'
"'Sure. So?'
"'Then shut up.'
"And I mean it because days fly by real fast. Soon we'll be as old as Donovan, but never as lonely, because Jeremiah has ok'ed school. For two nickel bags a week, plus dates with Felicia's friends on weekends after he does his homework, Jeremiah will give junior high an honest shake. I also threw in trying to hand over some of my damn luck to him. He said swell and also asked us not to call him small person anymore. You know, maybe my damn luck is spreading around all over us like some kind of terrific virus. Who the fuck really knows life or luck?

"That's it for the tape. I'll hide it under my bed. It's back to writing history one day, but not for a while just yet. See, tomorrow is another juicy Sunkist. We all take our places lining up getting the big bite from the orange, and we're all practically nodding out from vitamin C. No more tape.

"Good night and good-bye."

Aspects of Victor Cruz at Twenty-one

Victor was almost twenty-one.

The mailbox suddenly became very popular as testimonials and birthday cards stuffed in plump envelopes showed days in advance. Even on Victor's birthday, mail was still arriving. It was such an exciting and festive occasion (two communiques from the Home), that the brothers decided to purchase a birthday cake; however, the Carvel was closed. Still hyper with the excitement of real mail, José and Felipe toyed with the idea of jimmying open the bolted door while Jeremiah scrounged about for a brick to gain immediate entry. But since nobody was certain that such cakes were always in stock, the Cruzes ended up ambling back home. They did sing "Happy Birthday" and pounded Victor on the back and head until he almost got angry.

When they told him the Carvel was shut down, Victor only said, "Nice try." And he meant it, because there was no need for ice cream cake. All the recent mail had been like individual cupcakes specially baked for him. Far more important, the variety of letters and cards were surely the closest he'd ever get to the album José had longed for. Victor held up each piece of mail like prize booty and remembered the face and sound of each writer.

I. LINDA COHEN

I can still sketch Victor pacing up and down the narrow halls of the reception cottage. Each day he became more and more restless as our lazy staff decoded and studied his bewildering test scores. Victor was causing great commotion, for he had chewed woolly chunks from a newly carpeted foyer, gnawed the front desk legs, and immediately scribbled his city philosophy on many of the barren walls.

Once in Cottage A, Victor was immediately assigned to me. He was always very eager to be liked and miraculously resilient enough still to trust authority figures. On my first report I pointed out that he was very relieved to be out of the Bronx, but was deeply concerned about his brothers who were still with the mother. Also, Victor was incredibly hungry. Often he would bite his lips until they bled and then would lap up the blood like a happy vampire.

Though against the rules of the institution, I set out food for Victor each therapy session. As time passed, this practice continued and Victor then brought me snacks. In the beginning this proved distressing, for he was often caught stealing the food at the local supermarket. In time, Victor began doing maintenance work and handling several paper routes and so my presents were eventually honestly earned. To this day whenever I see chocolate-covered peanuts, I think of little hands offering a band of moist, melting candies.

ASPECTS OF VICTOR CRUZ AT TWENTY-ONE

Victor would call me when things were rotten at the cottage, and he would always phone each holiday season to wish my family a happy time. He took honest (no sign of jealousy) pleasure in my family situation, indeed he drew strength from a well-knit family. My own children and husband were quite fond of Victor, and then of his brothers when they, too, visited. But Victor was my favorite, though Felipe and José were always gentle and open to me, and Felipe would usually walk me to my car each afternoon like a private bodyguard checking the tires and the car to see if everything was ok.

When I moved to California, Victor called twice (I had encouraged him to do so) during crisis situations, but for the past eighteen months there have been no calls, just several enigmatic postcards.

I am so proud Victor has succeeded at the garage and, indeed, has become a conglomerate with his brothers running a thriving antique shoppe. I plan to visit their store before the year is out.

Oh Victor, to be twenty-one is a miracle of sorts. Much love and good wishes to all the Cruz boys.

2. SISTER NOREEN

Many things have changed at the Home. The cutoff age for troublesome wards is now sixteen, when a recalcitrant child can be dismissed and returned to the city. In complete candor, I doubt if Victor now would have remained with us past sixteen. Today we are staffed by laypeople, and present policy is very firm about those who will not quickly and easily adapt themselves to facing reality. There is far less stealing and pilferage at the Home and in nearby towns (acts for which our children were often correctly blamed), and many more of our children graduate the local high school. I feel the world in general has lost patience with orphans and wards, so they must toe the line very quickly.

Victor Cruz did graduate high school, but José and Felipe did not last, and my secretary reports that Jeremiah Cruz was never at Sacred Home, yet they are all part of our success story. We do not encourage Home graduates to remain in the county. We do not wish them to become at all dependent on our institution, yet the Cruz brothers have managed to become successful merchants in a nearby town. Surely Sacred Home must be given some share in their successful adaptation to society.

Therefore, on behalf of the institution and staff, I wish Victor Happy Birthday and continued success.

3. BILLY MURPHY

In my years at Cottage A, Victor stands out for what he didn't do. I mean, let's face it, the kid got into plenty of trouble. But he was never a troublemaker, wise-ass, or ringleader either. He had a chance to be all those things, but something or somebody was holding him back.

Vic had a calm air about him, and he could make dumb jokes so all the other kids admired him. In my high-school days our quarterback was always making with the gags. It was expected of a quarterback even if the jokes weren't funny. Vic saw that at Sacred Home if you were the main man then you were liable to be destroyed, so he stayed on the sidelines.

In fact, I forget the story exactly, but there was real

trouble at the high school his sophomore year, but Vic stepped back nice and easy, and everything blew away and was forgotten. Look, he wasn't chicken but, like I said, he was getting good advice and he had brought along with him this poise.... So I'm not surprised he's doing ok and, like me, is into repairing cars. I remember him in the machine shop listening to the teacher like some kind of serious pre-med student. See, it paid off.

Not too many teenagers around Sacred Home anymore. The bigger cottages, like A, are padlocked and never used. I went back last summer and it was a sad sight to see the deterioration. The grass was real high and there was all kinds of weeds ruining the playing fields. All the cottages needed paint jobs and the whole layout needed mowing and seeding. Boy, I can see Vic giving orders to kids big and small, really policing the area and getting it orderly. He had a favorite phrase—*neat and family*—he'd always say that.

Mostly when you say his name I remember how he made it easy for me most of the time in the cottage. I think I was fair to Vic and I always appreciated how he didn't give me much static.

I'm real glad he and his brothers stayed tight. Stayed neat and family, I mean.

4. PEDRO SANCHEZ

Dear Victor,

I still remember our underwear heist like it was yesterday. How we cleaned out all the Home jockey shorts, all sizes, how long we cased that damn laundry building, and picked off those stacked bundles at the right second. How you, me, and Ortega unloaded the loot at Ortega's cousin's outdoor clothing market. How he paid a nickel for each undie and we stuffed our faces with pizza, hot dogs, custard, and french fries. Boy, all the Sisters suspected us, but couldn't prove anything.

Remember how we planned to hit the high school music and media department: plenty of expensive stereos, TVs, and instruments easy to unload since Ortega's fat cousin knew every Bronx fence. Ortega said "First underwear, then the high school, and last, banks." And suddenly you were on your ass, slugged, or like you fell over something. You had a swollen jaw and a funny look in your eyes. Right after that you really changed, got conservative. You said banks were definitely out and even the high-school idea was too risky.

So Ortega and me tried it alone and a guard caught us and we got kicked out and warned to keep moving on or they'd bust us good. I missed you, Victor. You were always one straight guy. But the Home was always a drag. Still, it got worse until I got nailed in California. I was picking cherries last spring and got into a fight with my foreman one Saturday night. This time the bastard had friends and I had to use my knife, and one of his friends isn't around any more. It was sort of self-defense, but I'm rotting here while my lawyer appeals the fucking decision.

Here's my address; you can write me here. We'll talk about the good old times. We had some good troops, and some fun games and wars.

5. CONSUELA ORTIZ

Victor always confided in me. He told me his father was a ghost who'd been killed in a bank holdup years ago and now camped outside the Home watching over things and enjoying the country air. I never saw the ghost, and neither did José or Felipe, but Victor was always mumbling and arguing and sometimes laughing to himself many, many times. I'll tell you, at no time was Victor crazy, so if he believed he had an invisible friend, let him believe. It certainly saved him in tenth grade.

Tenth grade is the turning point for Home kids. That's the grade they drop out, but a few like me and Manuel and, crazy enough, Victor, kept on trucking. Tenth grade is when high school begins and it's when Home kids for the first time leave the grounds for more education. Quickly they become even more lost and sad. Few of us can read enough to pass the Regents and get the regular graduation certificate. Victor got a general diploma which means he didn't have to take the Regents. Even that was a miracle. But I remember Victor saying, "If only Poppa had an education, I could pass any damn tests."

You never saw prejudice like you did in high school. The other kids and all the teachers looked down on you. If you got a good mark, they either thought you cheated or you were a circus freak.

Even with the ghost around, Victor was in bad shape. We never were nothing but friends, and that is funny too, since in high school I lay with every Home kid who asked, and they *all* asked. But Victor really wanted talking and advising only. He didn't see any hope. I begged him to hold on. He said he'd try, but he was looking to do other things. Ortega and Sanchez were rowdy, tough kids, never up to any good, and they talked Victor into their gang. Sanchez and Ortega admired only Jesse James. Victor would have gone in with them, except one day walking to school he told me proudly, "You won't believe it, Consuela, but Poppa waled the shit out of me in front of Ortega and Sanchez."

"They saw him?"

"They saw me flying through the air and taking the

count. What a straight right! Poppa coulda been a flyweight contender, easy!"

I asked him if the ghost said anything.

"Poppa said, 'Jail and death, jail and death is all you'll get from those bums.'"

"Did he say anything about school?"

"Yeah, how did you know?"

"He's a father, right?"

"Right. Poppa said, 'Hold, hold on,' he kinda sang it."

And Victor did hold on. Manuel coached him; I did too. Victor more than held on. He graduated. And now he's twenty-one and into business. Manuel says one day the Cruzes will finance his political career.

Once Victor passed tenth grade, he had the chance. I hope whatever it is or was that whispered into Victor's ear is still there, helping out.

6. MANUEL ROSADO

When I run for political office my speeches will be very short. People don't want to hear. They want to see. Same now. Victor is a survivor. He survived the hard way. No one gave him a damn thing; no one really wished him to succeed. Even now, the tributes grudgingly handed out by the Home show they don't know how to say 'Good work'; they only know how to fuck over the kids and to promptly answer reports from the probation officers. Victor and Consuela had survived gang wars and gang bangs, incredible childhoods, and still they want more, because more might mean better if you can stay alive long enough. Society is very tricky. Someone like me can get to like very much the safety and easy comfort of libraries and to enjoy the power and prestige that higher and higher education gives you. And the protection you surely derive from more and more degrees. It is essential for me to always keep in touch with Consuela, and especially Victor and his brothers, for they are still at the edge of society.

I share their enthusiasm when I see how society, in its powerful silence, cannot wither all of us into vanishing, surrendering, or going on welfare, or being junkies. Victor is holding off society—he's about even in his struggle. I only hope I am fighting as hard and doing as well as fifty-fifty.

Bravo, Victor Cruz! May I greedily and often rip off some of your strength and purity. Bravo!

7. ANDREI KOUSITSKY

Victor is one in a million regardless of race, creed, or color. I'm prejudiced only concerning those persons who do not pay their rent and other due bills. Always Victor has taken the great pains to come up with what's due me, and when he was a little short, he apologized and quickly came up with the rest. He has a thing about his apartment, and you can tell how he's more than happy to pay for having such a cluttered place. I knew guiding him and his brothers in business would be a wise investment. Even his younger brothers are getting smart.

Happy Birthday, kid.

The Long Walk

No matter whether the dreams were long and elaborately concocted, or short but lucid, Raymondo Cruz died in each sequence. Dumped on by an avalanche of bullets, he kicked the bucket nightly. Therefore, it followed like the next leaky faucet drip, that there was no end to Raymondo Cruz's restlessness, hyper-squirming, and absolute inability to sleep. And during his lengthy days, the ghost was so incredibly weary there could be no heroic attempt to stand erect, even though Victor was always so childishly pleased when Poppa didn't crouch or slouch. Gaping holes in Raymondo's upper torso had widened as pus fringed each reopened wound. Despite his nightmares of unceasing death finales, the ghost of Raymondo Cruz had never felt more alive, since exquisite pain was always a devoted companion. Desperate for some relief, the ghost attempted smoking once more, but inhaling was absolute torture. The old man's feet were blistered, his ankles swollen, and his knees jiggled as if ruled by an unseen puppeteer's wires.

Victor tried to be sympathetic.

"Don't dream, Poppa! Use your willpower. Will no more dreams. If you can be a ghost, you can also get rid of the bad dreams."

"I came, not to complain, but to tell you how proud I am of you."

"Huh, Poppa, huh. . . . I can't hear, you're all bent over. Is it that bad?"

"I came to gloat over and be with you. Speaking into the magic tape or writing about all of us is fine, good, good Victor."

"What's fine?"

"Difficulties with words makes a sour tale sweet."

"Still don't get it. You look bushwhacked."

"I'm too tired to ever yawn again."

"Christ, lie down, Poppa."

"And on the tape," the ghost mumbled, "your unpleasant voice grates, but like a legend. Heroic!"

"Uh, uh," Victor warned. "We're no legend."

"Perhaps in time," the ghost said wearily, but sweetly.

"No fuckin' way, Poppa. To be a legend, you got to make real waves one day."

"So."

"Or be very lucky. Or lose real bad."

"All is not impossible," the father argued and waved limply.

Victor thought nastily, Who's he waving at? Does the old man think he's part of some Spic parade? Shit, he's far gone.

The father looked away in order to avoid continuing to read his son's thoughts.

"We're not overstepping, Poppa. I'm not kidding. This is the last word."

Poppa squinted ferociously and backed away.

"Don't fade out. Hear me good. I don't want, and we don't need, no new kind of pain, or too much action, or chancy fuck-ups. We got enough trouble with little Jeremiah Cruz. We only had to have you shot up and us abandoned to finally make it here. End of story."

Poppa nodded absently. "I merely honored your storytelling."

Victor scoffed and firmly warned, "No more legend crap."

Hurt and rebuffed and partially deposed, the ghost of Raymondo Cruz searched the neighborhood for any place to get some sleep and dismally failed.

To bolster and cement the rebuff, Victor gifted his brothers with a Pentax K1000 camera. José's dreams of countless snapshots for a photo album belatedly arrived. Jeremiah delighted in taking the family pictures.

"None of me, bros! That way when yours sincerely gets famous, the cops will never have nothing for their files. Hey, Felipe, try and smile, ya big turkey. Good, that's close enough. Wow, *Jaws* or what?"

With the purchase of a camera, Victor had sworn off any more words on paper or mouthing off any new potential legendary narrative, so the notebook and tape recorder were filed away.

Even if the technicians had known of the challenge of photographing a ghost and had been equal to a surreal solution, the family portrait would not have included Raymondo Cruz. The old man was a definite no-show, as he hiked hopelessly in all directions. During his aimless wanderings, however, Raymondo Cruz's feet finally toughened up and the ballooned ankles deflated, plus the ghost began to experience essential first-rate visions. He could hear the marvelous moan of long-dead trains sweeping great mountains and arching great rivers and valleys. He could also detect the siren call of boats sounding in foggy water; could taste the salty spray from spitting oceans. And he came up with a new slogan, *Upstate is best.* Raymondo dawdled for many additional days and weeks until the hallucinations coalesced into a more unified pattern and he could settle for a practical solution. Finally there was the proper mix, the clatter of mighty trains, the smell of raunchy seas, the creaking of great ships pushing through angry oceans, the booming sound of a megaphoned voice, and the voice of a long-dead Cortez salesman promising the better life upstate, maybe.

Walking with genuine resolution, the ghost of Raymondo Cruz discovered himself in more familiar surroundings. He was not flitting up the stairs returning to his sons. There was no standing ovation or even token applause. It was four in the morning and they were all snoring loudly. For one perfect moment, Poppa was engulfed by a great smothering love that caused a choking spasm, bringing the old man to his knees. A different vibe floated toward him. Raymondo watched as it sailed away but doggedly returned, hovering expectantly: Raymondo prepared to accept the apparition, a puffball, and rising firmly to his feet lunged forward to volley. Haloes and sensational rainbows darted on all sides of the spongy sphere, and Raymondo wisely saw this puffball also symbolized the love left over for him in this apartment. And the ghost accepted remaindered love graciously and sent the ball back over the torn, shredded net. The love was of and for a distant beloved relative, and when the ball floated by a third time, Poppa did not even think of spiking it, but rather sent it right back softly and gently into play.

Then the ghost of Raymondo Cruz yawned for the first time in four months. Exhilarated and pleased by the sudden yawn, Poppa roamed about the slightly unfamiliar rooms looking for Victor. Mucho trembled in his sleep and then growled once. Poppa stumbled over furniture twice before finally finding his quarry. Yawning steadily now, the ghost tried to awaken Victor. He tugged and tugged at the boy's feet and yanked at Victor's pajama tops. His son, however, snored on. Over Raymondo's right shoulder the ball, now shrinking in size, but turning and spinning like a small planet, glowed with a pleasant and eerie neon light.

Finally Raymondo kicked Victor gently, then kicked harder aiming for his son's ass, but nailing him in the small of his back.

"Fuck, wha . . ."

"It's time."

"Poppa, what time is it?"

"Time."

"Yow, it's pitch black out there."

"Victor."

"Long time no see, Poppa. Really glad you're back. We'll talk later."

"Victor, the lousy dreams are maybe gone."

"Great! G'night Poppa. Later."

Raymondo Cruz booted his son one more time.

"Hey, hey, take it easy, huh? That smarts."

"Also my son, wear a sweater, it's chilly at four in the morning."

"Believe me, nothing is happening at four, Poppa. Can't it wait? I gotta be in the garage at seven, you know that."

"Wear shoes, not sneakers," the ghost cautioned, then advised, "It's moist out."

"Fuck. You buggin' out, Poppa."

But Victor got dressed and lugged on his combat boots. The ghost was at the open front door. Victor headed toward him and then Poppa ran down the stairs.

Poppa usually walked slowly in a sideways shuffle. Today it was like the old man was in a damn race. Victor had to jog to get alongside his fast-moving Poppa who looked surprised to see him. God, Poppa was increasingly forgetful. Still, it was sweet to have him back once more.

"Thank you, Victor, but I have to come to terms with myself."

"OK," Victor yawned and mumbled.

"True, isn't it, Victor?"

"Huh."

"We have never walked before."

"Why this morning, Poppa?"

"Because."

The ghost of Raymondo Cruz mouthed *because* like a boss of bosses, so Victor easily accepted the stubborn tone, and he saw it was useless to ask why any longer. Especially since he was jogging this very minute along deserted streets with a bullet-ridden ghost on absolutely barren streets where not a cat or a water rat streaked by, and where there wasn't even a garbage can around. It was empty, man, empty out, except for the two of them. Poppa's hi-top sneakers were caked with mud and dried blood.

"We go through town."

"To where?" Victor questioned.

"To the Thruway entrance."

"You look lousy, Poppa. Maybe we shouldn't be moving so fast."

"Of course I feel lousy, but we must go fast. You have the job at seven."

"Maybe you caught a bug. The flu is going around."

"What I need is a visit with Estrella."

That comment made Victor wince and run past his father. Victor sullenly waited under the next lamppost for the ghost to catch up. A few buttons of Raymondo's polo had sprung open. It was up to Victor to button up his old man.

"Shit, Estrella is just another dime-a-dozen gypsy hooker."

"She's your goddamned godmother, so watch your mouth carefully."

"Truth is truth, dirt is dirt."

"No matter, she is a deep individual. Estrella can predict the future. In the old days she always predicted my failures."

"That was easy, Poppa."

"She spouted awful secrets. If you curled your right wrist she could tell from the wrinkles the date and place of your death."

"I ain't curling shit."

"And I'm sure Estrella would notice and agree how I'm getting younger, more childish as you, my sons, mature like good grapes."

"Ghosts can't change that much."

"They can."

"Hey, you've had these bummer trips before and then all of a sudden you get smarter and happier than ever."

"This lead load is heavy on me. Yet it doesn't bother me. I have accepted this new decree. I think, I think I'm ready," the ghost calypsoed.

"Maybe it's only in your head."

Through the very long, the very boring, and seemingly endless uncomfortable walk, Poppa hissed, steamed, moaned, and even sang a little. Victor kept his mouth shut and his eyes lowered, intent only on matching the ghost stride for goddamned stride. Near the end, the ghost of Raymondo Cruz reached out for Victor, who alertly and firmly grasped the fragile soft-boned hand. They walked awhile holding hands, but still made little conversation. When the dirty gray sky started to lighten up and birds commenced singing, and a car actually passed them, Raymondo Cruz started talking again. Victor had been daydreaming about buying his father an elegant old cane. If the old man was now into long, long walks, he should have the cane for support and company.

But Poppa, easily reading his eldest son's thoughts, croaked out in a hoarse whisper, "Forget the cane, but you know, Victor, once I would have liked..."

"What? Go on."

"Aah, nah, forget it."

"Nah, don't forget it. José still bugs me for more stuff about you and what you still say. C'mon, it's important."

"Very well. You tell José I would've liked a dog."

"A damn dog!"

"That was in my early manhood, when I first married Momma. I longed to be..."

Victor waited.

"But don't laugh, my son."

"Go on, Pop."

"A dog walker."

"You mean walk mutts for a price."

"No, not some mutt, but a fine and beautiful animal. And I would smile and nod to others like me, dog walkers. Later on we would all get to be friends, the dogs and their owners. All of us."

"We got Mucho."

"I longed for just the normal high-priced dog. Enough of freaks!"

"Right."

"My dream was to walk this dog four, five times a

day, and love it and speak to it like a dear friend and child. We would have only good times in all the parks."

"I can dig that."

"My other dream was to take the carriages with all of you as babies in them and this dog at my side, and we would walk and walk so far that the Bronx was no more."

Victor didn't argue.

"You're sweating, my son."

"I could use a beer."

"Here's the Thruway."

"Now let's turn back," Victor sighed.

"*You* turn back."

"You'll be coming back soon?"

"The long walk is over. Thank you for joining me," the ghost said formally.

"Poppa, look, I'll take a day off. I'll spend the whole day with you. We can bull and dream all day."

"Each day is a trap for Cruzes. Go to work, Victor. I'm going."

"Where?"

"Upstate."

The ghost of Raymondo Cruz pinched, goosed, kissed, patted Victor good-bye and repeated that the idea of a cane was beautiful but inappropriate, and to forget it. Victor finally grudgingly took off. But after a few blocks he retraced his steps and headed for a grassy knoll overlooking the Thruway where he could see his father, the ghost of Raymondo Cruz, standing erect, grimly smiling, his right thumb angled, clearly requesting a hitch as car after truck after car sped on by. Poppa was under a sign saying BUFFALO 450 MILES. He kept up his classic stance and was not put off by the relentless flow of no-stops. In fact, Poppa looked very optimistic and not at all tired. By the time he got back home, Victor had decided to find an antique cane anyway. Any heartfelt gesture is significant and a possible final useless gesture is surely the most important of all.